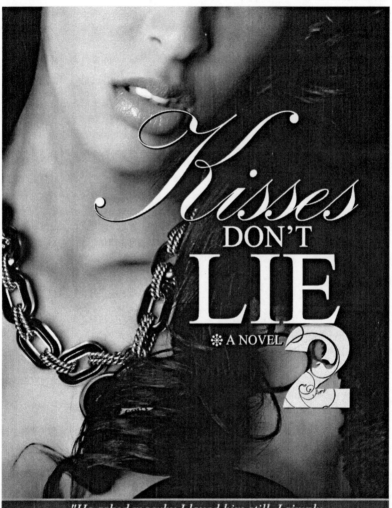

"He asked me why I loved him still. I simply told him he used to make me smile."

TAMIKA NEWHOUSE

Author of *Will Love Ever Know Me*

Kisses Don't Lie 2 by Tamika Newhouse

Delphine Publications focuses on bringing a reality check to the genre urban literature.
All stories are a work of fiction from the authors and are not meant to depict, portray, or represent any particular person.

Names, characters, places, and incidents are either the product of the author's imagination or are used fictitiously, and any resemblances to an actual person living or dead are entirely coincidental.

ISBN 13 - 978-0984692392

Edited by Alanna Boutin
Cover Design: Odd Ball Designs
Layout: Write On Promotions

Published by Delphine Publications
www.DelphinePublications.com

Printed in the United States of America

Acknowledgements

I must say that the six years I have spent on this journey is unbelievable and just as amazing as when I very first started. I want to thank and acknowledge my Lord whom I grow closer with each day for his continue covering of my life and family. I am grateful for being able to live out my purpose and that is to write.

Special thank you to my family Dajiah and Marckus, mama loves you both. And Senior thanks to you for not only being that person to help build me up but also for being my backbone. To Annie and Uncle Gary thank you for always allowing me to let my hair down and escape from the world whenever I am in Houston. Nicola, thank you for being that immediate shoulder and consistent listening ear.

Last but not least thank you Granny, who is my last living grandparent for always supporting me. You are the only one in my family that has read every one of my books and my company, Delphine's books. That means so much to me.

In the world of business special thanks to Alanna Boutin, Davida Baldwin, Christina S. Brown, Latoya Smith, Tory Butler, and every book club and reader that has ever supported me. I am very bad at remembering everyone but for those who genuinely care for me, thank you for being that motivation for me.

In remembrance to my mother Delphine and my big mama Virginia Harris, may you rest in peace and continue to be that overseer I so very need.

As you turn the pages into Kisses Don't Lie 2, welcome to my world for now. Sit back kick up your feet and get lost in a world of drama and pure entertainment.

Kisses from

Tamika

Dedicated to my son Marckus
whom tends to always make me smile

Kisses Don't Lie 2

David kindly agreed and got out of his seat. As I watched him walk out the door I stood up from my seat and marched over to Chris.

Standing across from him at the table he sat at, I folded my arms across my chest and said, "So you made the move, huh?"

He smiled again and said, "I let you get away before, but this time, I'm not going to let you go that easily."

I couldn't help but to smile as I read his expression as he declared his love for me. I loved this man, but as soon as I wanted to say how happy I was to see him, Dean, and then Keith, popped in my head. I knew I had to make a choice on what I was going to do and quick.

"Are you serious?" I asked.

"I'm sitting here, aren't I?" Chris was a secret affair I had craved back in college. One passionate kiss led to a decade of feelings that I never acted out on. Mainly because he was the brother to the man I had promised to be with. But being with Dean was out of the question now that his wife tried to kill me. I would be a fool to try to be with him after that.

I plopped myself down in chair right in front of him and just stared for a moment. I smiled, and then he smiled. No words were spoken. I blew out air and poked my bottom lip out as if I was preparing to throw a tantrum. "I can't say no to you, Chris."

He leaned forward in his seat and licked his lips before saying, "I'm not here to make you love me. You just simply do." His words didn't make me cringe or shy away. Because he was right; I did love him.

Brittany

I COULDN'T BREATHE. I was huffing and puffing so hard my insides felt like they were sitting in the middle of my throat. I rolled over onto the other side of the bed to readjust the way I was lying when Tionna came marching into my room. "OK, Ms. Mary Poppins, do you need help in here?"

"Tionna, not right now, OK? This baby is giving me the blues, and I am ready for this sucker to come out."

Tionna laughed and rolled her eyes. "At five months preggers, oh, you'll be waiting all right. Little Mikey ain't ready to come out."

I rolled my eyes and reminded her that my son wasn't going to be a junior. "Why not, Brit Brat? Name that boy after his daddy."

Kyla

I WOULD NEVER admit that I ran from my problems. But then again, we can lie to ourselves the best. No wonder I was sitting here listening to this man talk a good game. I don't know what the hell he was saying, but he looked good saying it. I had to block his good looks out of my mind, because since making partner, it was my duty to keep personal and business separated. That is, besides Keith.

Hmmm, just thinking about Keith gets me wet right now. I love to feel that man in between my legs, and for a damn good reason too. He's good at what he does. But who was I fooling? I was torn.

Trying to take my mind off of my own issues I took my attention back to my colleague, David, a junior partner in my marketing firm along with myself. He offered to take me out for drinks since he was new to D.C. and didn't know anyone here. I guess I wanted to be nice. Being nice was going to get me in trouble as I sipped slowly on my Long Island. I couldn't get tipsy and not be accountable for my actions with Mr. Sexy. Plus, having sex with one man in the office was good enough.

I felt my phone vibrate in my pocket as I gave David a one-second signal as I checked to see who it was. I pressed the menu button and saw his name flash across my screen. CHRIS!

It was a text from the man I ran away from. The man I knew I couldn't be with because I had unfinished business with his brother Dean. Ugh, and how could I forget Dean? My very first love. But that shit ended in a nightmare after the wife—which he failed to mention—came after me and tried to shoot my ass. No, literally, she tried to kill me. That's why she's sitting in jail now. Seven years before her crazy ass gets out. Thank goodness.

I glanced at my phone again and gave David an uncomfortable smile as the message said, LOOK BEHIND YOU.

Turning slowly in my seat inch by inch, I scrutinized the restaurant. And then . . . there he sat. He smiled and reached for his phone again.

My phone vibrated as I knew he sent another text message. Blowing out hot air as I thought I left my problems back in Texas, I looked at my phone to see it say, I'M READY TO BE WITH YOU WHEN YOU ARE, AND IF IT MEANS MAKING D.C. MY NEW HOME, THEN SO BE IT.

Sulking in my seat as I turned back around to face David, I slowly said, "Can we call it a night? I just saw someone I know, and I know it's going to be a long night."

"Look, I don't have time for this. I got to get up and go to work."

Now Tionna was the one huffing and puffing and rolling her eyes. "Michael gives you more than enough money; he put a bid on a house for you, and your stubborn ass still won't quit that sorry-ass receptionist job."

"Why would I?" I asked, rolling out of bed to find my clothes for work. I had told Tionna and my mother on more than one occasion that Michael doesn't owe me anything. So everything that he is giving today he can take away tomorrow, and then where would I be?

"You need to trust that man, Brittany. He loves you."

I knew Tionna was right. He showed me he loved me every day. But I know men and all men are the same deep down. Michael may want to do right, but he is a man, and men falter like a motherfu—Tionna called out my name interrupting my thought.

"Brittany!"

"What, heifer? Damn, I'm getting dressed."

"Never mind, I'll just let you be hardheaded."

I walked out of my closet with my shoes in tow and said, "Thanks for butting out of my business."

"Ugh, that baby has you mean as hell. Call me when you get off of work. I'm out." She got up from her seat, walked over, and kissed me on the cheek before leaving. I embraced her gesture, and then put on my work shoes when I heard her call my name.

I yelled out as I got up from where I was sitting to walk toward my apartment living room. "What, Tionna? I thought you were gone."

Tionna stood there with my front door open. I noticed someone standing on the opposite side of my door and began to stand on my tippy toes to see who it was over her shoulder.

Tionna's expression had me raising one eyebrow in concern. Whoever it was, she didn't seem to be happy to see them. "Who are you?" Tionna held a lot of attitude in her question as I finally saw the face of who it was. *Oh, she's cute. Wonder who that is.*

I wobbled over to stand next to Tionna as the woman began to speak. "Hi, there, is Brittany home?"

"I don't know you to be coming over and just asking for someone, and we don't know you. You do own a phone, right?" Tionna interrogated her again. I didn't understand why Tionna was being so rude to her. Then again as Tionna was asking the question I was thinking the same thing. *How does she know me?*

Making it to the doorway I stood next to Tionna and got an easy view of the short woman. She was clearly around my age in her midtwenties. Her extensions were long and curly with a hint of red streaks. She was cute, has a small buttonlike nose and big brown eyes. Her skin was blemish-free and just as golden as the sun.

As I looked her over my eyes trailed down to her belly. *Oh, she's pregnant.* "I'm Brittany, what's up?" I butted in. My curiosity was running thin.

The lady smiled and looked at me and said, "You are a cutie." I frowned with a mixture of being flattered but was uncomfortable at the same time.

Tionna raised up her hand and said, "Miss, if you don't mind, who are you? Are you selling something or what?"

She giggled and waved her hand off at us in a friendly gesture. "Oh, I'm sorry. I'm being rude. I was simply coming to meet Brittany. I mean, I couldn't wait to meet you because we have something in common." She looked down toward my stomach and pointed, "I can tell you're in your second trimester, huh?"

I nodded my head and gave her a slow, confused yes. "And you are?"

She extended her hand and said, "I am LeAnn. Sorry to be so rude. I just entered my second trimester too."

Tionna shrugged her shoulders and said, "Whoopty do. What's up? How do *we* know you?"

"Oh, you don't. I was actually asked not to seek out and talk to you, but I thought it was only fair. You see, we have something in common," LeAnn continued.

I added, "Yes, you said that before, and what is the common ground that we so happen to both be standing on?" This girl was getting more weird by the minute, and I could tell Tionna was about to go off.

She looked down at her belly, then to mine before looking back up at my face and said, "Our babies. They will have the same father."

Chris

WASHINGTON, D.C. WAS quite new to me, but I was determined to make the most out of it. Plus, I was hoping soon enough Kyla would want to move back to Texas anyway. Day two here I go, and I was out and about looking for work while Kyla was at her job. She had made partner now. And when she told me of this I knew I had to go ahead and make the move to D.C.

The only hard part was commuting back and forth to see my teenage daughter. But the distance between my brother and me was much needed. You see, I was in love with his first love. I was the reason why they never ended up back together. And lastly Kyla is that reason why I disregarded my relationship with my brother and pursued happiness with her instead.

Kyla and my brother Dean were done now anyhow. It only took Dean's now ex-wife Fiona to try to shoot Kyla to finally end their never-ending back-and-forth relationship. And for once I could openly be with the woman I have loved since that very first kiss.

Now, here I was clear across the country making the same journey Kyla did, away from Fort Worth, Texas, in the same pursuit of happiness. And I was determined to be happy. Today was long and draining. Kyla allowed me to stay with her last night, and it was perfect, but I knew I would have to get my own space.

After submitting six job applications, I decided to head to a local Starbucks in an effort to write. That was my true passion. I was going to finish my novel once and for all and finally land that book deal I've always dreamed about. And I needed that book deal more than ever. My savings was only going to last for so long.

After making it into the café, I ordered my usual and found a secluded spot. I pressed power on my laptop, and as I waited for it to power up I searched my surroundings. This place known as Chocolate City wasn't so bad. I was taking it all in.

The fast-paced life, congested traffic, cafés, and poetry lounges were everywhere . . . and black people. Black people of all shades and backgrounds were everywhere. I loved the vibe of this city. *I could get used to this.*

Taking a sip of my coffee I looked up and noticed a mixed couple. Something else I would have to get used to. There were a lot of different cultures here. Definitely a culture shock if you ask me. Being a Southern man, black folks in the South tended to act a certain way. But here, black folks and white folks blended together more, lived in lower housing divisions together, and I witnessed the lack of judgment toward my people here.

I still felt cautious about how to carry myself around these Northerners; but I was going to lean on Kyla to help me adjust to this new life. But just looking at this couple I couldn't help but smile. Not because I was happy for them, but just like them, I could openly rub Kyla's shoulder, kiss the back of her hand, or whisper sweet nothings into her ear.

I was happy-jealous right now. I decided to pick up my cell phone and noticed it was lunch time. I powered down my laptop and decided to walk the three blocks to Kyla's building. I wanted to see the woman I loved so much.

βββ

I was carrying two bags of food from a local sandwich shop that was a block away and riding the elevator up to the fifteenth floor. I was embarrassed to admit that I was anxious to surprise Kyla at work. I wanted to see what it is that she does. To see her in action at something that she loved excited me.

As the doors swung open I marched over to the receptionist desk and asked for Kyla Howard. The receptionist quickly dialed Kyla's extension. I could hear her voice through the receiver. "You may go in, sir. It's the third door on the left."

I nodded my head thanks as I made my way back and looked over her office space and the clear view of the busy streets of D.C. I knocked twice on her door and said, "Hey, babe."

She looked up from her desk and smiled. That smile alone made my heart swell. Her eyes held a genuine light in them, as if she was truly excited to see me. I wanted to look into her eyes for the rest of my life.

"Hey, handsome, what do you have here?" she asked, pushing her chair back from her desk and marching over toward me.

She wore a two-piece lime-colored skirt set that was mere inches from cutting off her circulation throughout her body. I could see every curve of her body as my eyes failed to stay in their sockets.

"Damn, babe, really, must you look this damn good in public?"

She laughed, grabbing the sandwich bags out of my hands and turned around to go back toward her desk. I ran up behind her wrapping my arms around her waist, kissing the back of her neck, and pressing my groin against her ass. And her ass felt like a missing puzzle piece against me. Perfect fit.

She laughed and said, "OK, OK, OK, now, Chris, back up. This is my office, and, plus, we didn't get a chance to talk about something I've needed to say for a while since you just surprised me yesterday with showing up and all."

She pointed for me to sit down in the chair before her desk as she walked back toward her front door and closed it. I could tell this was going to be a speech I didn't necessarily want to hear.

"OK, lay it on me. What's the bad news?" My eyes followed her as she made her way back toward me and sat down on top of her desk inches away from me.

"I have to be honest, Chris. Once I left Fort Worth, I was determined to believe that we were done. I mean, you were in Texas, and I was here. So when you stated you were going to come,

I brushed it off, and in that time frame, I carried out a relationship with someone else."

I raised an eyebrow. "Excuse me?" I tried to not sound upset because here she was clearly being honest with me.

"I'm sorry, Chris, but I didn't believe you. I mean, I have been lied to before time and time again, and now I'm stuck because I don't want to hurt anyone."

"OK, well, what are you trying to say?"

"I'm dating someone in my office. I have been since before I left for my vacation to Fort Worth this past summer, and it's been good for me. I haven't dated anyone in months. Maybe a year."

"But you love me, Kyla. Do you love him?" She grew quiet. I dropped my head down to fight the anger that was itching to burst out of me.

"I'm sorry, I really am. But I'm going to handle it OK. I'm going to make my decision." Kyla tried to sound like that was good news.

"Kyla, I moved out here to be with you." I placed my hands over my temples. "I waited ten years for this, Kyla. Do you think I am going to let you go that easily?" She grew quiet.

"I know, Chris. This I know."

"Who is he? I'm not going to do anything, Ky. You know that. I just want to know."

"His name is Keith, and he is a partner in this firm, which is why I have to be so careful about this. I just became partner here, and I can't start any drama."

As I opened my mouth to speak, a knock interrupted me. Kyla immediately jumped up to answer it. And I knew she was anxious to open the door because she wanted to avoid this conversation. Hell, to be honest, I didn't want to have this conversation either.

With my head still held down, my thoughts were interrupted when I heard laughter ring through the silence that was heavy in the air.

"Hey, girly, I came to bring you lunch." I heard the tone of a Spanish woman.

"Oh, girl, I didn't know you had food already. I will just go take it to your boo Keith and see if he wants it."

Next, I heard a male voice jump into their conversation and say, "You'll see if Keith wants what?"

Kyla and the Spanish woman laughed as the woman continued. "You want this baked potato? I was going to give it to Kyla, but she has food already. Oh and company. Hey, there!"

Deciding not to be rude I stood up and turned around to greet Kyla's friends. I cocked my head to the side as I stared in disbelief.

Kyla did the formal introduction, and I could sense some nervousness in her tone as she was about to introduce me to the man she just told me she was also in love with. "Keith, Gloria, this is one of my friends from my hometown. He's thinking about relocating here," Kyla said.

Gloria extended her hand and said, "Oh, hey, Chris, welcome to D.C. If you need any advice on where to live, ask Keith here. He knows everything."

I shook her hand, and then I reluctantly shook Keith's hand. "Keith, pleasure man. And, Gloria, who might I ask are you to Kyla?"

"Only her best friend since college," she laughed.

I stood there and listened to the three of them talk as I noticed Kyla wanting them to leave her office. But I was curious. I needed them to stay. At some point I heard Kyla ask, "Girl, why are you so hyper right now?"

Gloria laughed and said, "Oh, I just left Starbucks and had a double espresso. You know me. I need something to get me past this boring-ass Tuesday." She blew a kiss in the air and sashayed away as Keith kissed Kyla on the lips and left as well, but not before offering to take me out with some of his friends. I had agreed to go out because the more I knew about this Keith the better.

Besides, if I was going to tell Kyla that my competition was actually dating her friend Gloria, then I would need more evidence. The minute they both walked into this office, I knew, hands-down, that they were the couple I had just seen in Starbucks. Just my luck, huh?

Michael

I HAD TO end the day early. I canceled my last two meetings with two agents for the NBA and was now sprawled across my bed. I knew I only had about two hours before I made my routine drive over to Brittany's job to check in on her.

I loved that stubborn woman who refused to quit her job even after I put an offer up on a house for her. I was giving her everything she needed, and more, but she was too independent to accept what I was giving her for our child.

Only a matter of time I was sure and I would have her taking everything that I wanted to give her, plus more. I knew deep down that this was my moment to finally settle down and stop with the dating scene. Brittany just had to see for herself that I was ready.

I rolled over at the sound of my cell phone ringing and an unsaved number popped up. I pressed TALK and said, "Hello?"

"Finally," I heard her say as she blew her breath onto the phone.

I grunted in annoyance as I said, "Yes, LeAnn, what is it now?"

"Why are you acting like this, Michael? You know we are expecting." I rolled my eyes at her announcement again. Something just didn't add up with the woman I had an affair with almost three months ago. And to say I was fed up with her antics was putting it lightly; I was on the verge of getting a restraining order before I had to put my hands on her.

"Fuck!" I yelled. "What the hell do you want, woman?"

There was silence until she finally said, "You. I want you, Michael, and I want you to take responsibility for what is ours."

"Who is he?"

"Who?" she asked curiously.

"The man who got you pregnant, LeAnn. Stop fucking with me, a'ight? I am not in the mood for this today. I have other things to do." I hated that I had to use foul language toward a woman. That just wasn't me. But LeAnn brought the worst out of me.

"He is nobody but you."

"*One* time we had sex, LeAnn, and with protection, and your dates aren't adding up with your pregnancy. Now, it doesn't take a rocket scientist to put two and two together. You're trying to trap me, but one thing you must know, I'm not that easy to get over."

"Trap you? No, sweetheart, I just want to be treated right, and I thought your girl should know this too. I mean, she deserves to know too, don't you think?"

I paused and held my breath as I replayed the words she just said over in my head. "What?"

"You heard me."

I swallowed hard as I tried to think back over things I must have said to LeAnn in the past. *She must have found out about Brittany.* Why didn't it dawn on me that if LeAnn stalked me for this long that she would surely have found out about Brittany by now? I dropped my head in my hand and said, "What did you tell her?"

I could tell LeAnn was smiling as she said slowly, "Everything!" I clicked the phone shut just as I heard her begin to laugh.

Squeezing my eyes tightly I tried to block out the conversation I had just had with LeAnn. *This can't be happening!* Brittany and I were finally good now. She was carrying our child, whom she once wanted to abort, and now I'm faced with having to confess I slept with someone else who now claims I am the father of her child.

How was I going to get Brittany to believe me? I fell back on my bed and tried to fight the angry tears that were threatening to surface.

I heard a knock on my door after what I am guessing was a ten-minute mental debate. "What?" I yelled at the door.

"Bro, open up!" My brother Omar's voice came through my door as I rose up and jogged toward it.

I swung open the door, and Omar's expression changed from cool to concern. "Bro, what's up? Bad day?" He walked in, making his way to sit in front of my TV with his takeout.

I slammed the door and said, "LeAnn found Brittany."

Omar's stride stopped as he turned around to face me. "Damn, bro, what did Brittany say?"

I started to speak, but then it dawned on me. Brittany hadn't called me. Was that good or bad? "She hasn't called," I announced.

Omar blew out hot air and sat down on the couch. Searching his face for answers I asked, "What does that mean, bro, if she hasn't called?"

"One thing, Mike. She believes ole girl." He grabbed the remote and propped up his feet and called out, "Yo, bring me a beer. The game is about to start." I looked at him and balled my fist, wanting to aim my anger toward him.

"Dude, fuck the game! My girl is what's on my mind." I rushed past where he sat, grabbed my keys, and walked out the door without saying another word. I had to see her face to face before what LeAnn told her became her truth.

Gloria

I TURNED DOWN the burner on the oven and raised the lid up on my dumplings I had simmering in the pot. The salty spices ran havoc on my senses as I was anxious to get that first bite. It was late, and Victor wasn't home as he was working late, as usual. I grabbed my beer and took another swallow as I made my way to the patio.

When the fall breeze hit my skin I exhaled. I enjoyed being home alone, but I was bored. Who was I fooling? I needed some human contact, and I preferred Keith's over Victor's any day. I shook my head to knock Keith out of my thoughts and to turn my attention on my dying garden.

Mostly everything around my house was being neglected, including my husband. My best friend, Kyla, who had just made partner at our firm, was too busy to notice how unhappy at home I was, or the fact that I wanted and needed her man, Keith. I sat down on my chaise longue and threw my head back to fight the tears that wanted to say hello.

I wasn't happy, and I didn't know how to change that. With my eyes closed, I jerked at the sound of my phone ringing. I picked it up on the third ring. "Yes!"

"In a funky mood?"

"Maybe. What's up, Nadine?"

"Keith wants you over tonight. Can you get past Victor?"

My heart skipped a beat at the sound of Keith's name, even if it was coming from the lips of his girlfriend of ten years and now his wife. "What time?"

"One hour. Don't be late. You know he hates that, and wash up. Last time I could have sworn I tasted another man on you. You know that's not allowed."

I rolled my eyes and sucked my teeth. "I'm always clean for my Keith."

"Excuse me?" Nadine interrupted me. I bite my bottom lip, hating the fact that slipped out of my mouth. Nadine continued, "Gloria, let me remind you that you are a sexual desire for him, nothing more. He fucks you, but he wifes me. Never get the lines crossed because you will *never* have my place."

"I'll be there in one hour." I clicked the phone off before she could continue. I smirked at the thought of Nadine declaring Keith as hers because she thought I only had Keith in the bedroom but failed to know my girl Kyla actually owned his heart. That was the one thing I hated about Kyla.

βββ

I was at a loft Keith borrowed from time to time from the partners at the firm. It was set in downtown D.C. on the thirty floor of its building. The scenery was beautiful. You could see the National Mall from where I stood to the beaming lights of the city and skyscrapers.

Dressed in satin peach-colored lingerie, I stood in front of the window admiring the view, sipping on red wine as I waited for Keith and Nadine to arrive.

The room was quiet until I suddenly heard footsteps near the front door. I became anxious as I hurried over to the bed; set my glass on the table, and sat down in the middle of the bed. The plush fabric formed itself around my ass, causing the heat that was rising from my sweet nectar to trail down to my inner thighs.

My eyes locked in on the doorknob as it began to turn. I heard a male grunt as he appeared from behind the door. I jumped up and said, "Who are you?"

Only standing about five foot five, dark, slim, and dreads down to his shoulders, he said, "Keith and Nadine sent me. Why?"

I walked over to the chair next to the bed and reached for my robe when he said, "Don't cover up. It's a part of the game they say."

I raised an eyebrow and said, "Game? I'm confused."

He walked over to me and handed me a piece of paper. I hurriedly opened it, nervous and scared at the same time. I was standing in a room half-naked with a man I didn't even know.

I WANT TO SEE YOU PLEASE HIM. I LOVE TO WATCH.

I looked at the note from front to back and said, "What the hell?"

"So are you ready?" he asked, taking a step toward me.

I held my hands up and said, "Wait! So Keith wants me to fuck you?"

"That's the plan, and he's watching you right now. I'm guessing you don't want to disappoint him." My eyes traveled across the room to see if I saw a camera. I didn't. I closed my eyes to fight back the tears and fear as my bottom lip quivered.

"So, are you ready?" he asked again.

My eyes popped open as I stared at him. *OK, girl, he isn't ugly, and if Keith wants you to, then go right ahead.* I slowly nodded my head yes as he walked toward me. My heart began to race uncontrollably.

Only a mere few inches away from me, he placed his hands on both of my shoulders forcing me downward. "Give him a good show, Mama," he whispered.

On my knees, he took his hands and began to unbuckle his pants. A tear escaped my eyes as the reality of this thing was setting in. Pulling himself out, he brushed his tip across my lips and said, "Open up." Jabbing himself in my mouth, I cried out, but I didn't budge. I closed my eyes and pretended it was the man I loved. Keith. It was him that wanted this anyway, and I would do anything to please him. So I put on my best show.

Kyla

I CLICKED THE phone off with Keith after canceling our date just as Chris was appearing in my bedroom door. I blew out hot air as the reality of my living situation was setting in. I was dating one man now and living with another.

"Hey you!" Chris said.

"Hey, what's up?" I asked borderline annoyed. I wasn't annoyed by him though, just the current bad timing.

"Am I bothering you?" he asked with his head tilted and slightly concerned.

"No, Chris, come on in; take a seat. Tell me what you did today," I said, trying to lighten the mood.

He walked in dressed in a casual shirt and shorts. His mannerism was screaming throughout the room. His presence always made me moist as he stood there, unaware of the affect he had on my body at this very moment. He had swag and with a genuine heart he equaled danger for heart.

"I applied for a few positions and wrote in my book today." He took a seat inches away from me on my bed.

The mentioning of his book made me smile brightly. *A man who wrote—ugh! He was a triple threat.* "Why are you single again?" I laughed out.

He calmly said, "I'm not." He hinted toward me. I purposely overlooked his comment and proceeded with my casual conversation.

"Your book, what is it about?"

"It's about a man who once loved and lost it due to making a bad decision. It's kind of like an autobiography."

I deflected my eye contact and turned it toward my cell phone that was buzzing. It was a message from Gloria saying she needed to talk. I tilted my head to the side with concern.

"Are you OK?" Chris asked watching me.

"Ummm, yeah. It's just Gloria texting me saying she needs to talk to me. It's an odd, random message that has me concerned."

"Can you text her and let her know you are available tomorrow? I have something I want to do to you tonight. I mean, for you," he laughed.

My smile spread wide as I focused in on his obvious joke. "OK, I can do that just this once."

I texted her back to meet me at Brown Sugar's in the a.m. for breakfast before work. She agreed. I dropped the phone on my bed and said, "OK, Mr. Chris, I'm all yours."

"No, you're not, but soon will be." He reached for my hand and led me out of my bedroom and down my stairs.

I followed him in my den and upon turning the corner I could tell my fireplace was lit. I noticed a pallet on the floor and a bowl of popcorn with a box of Sugar Babies candy and two cans of sweet tea. I laughed shyly at his gesture.

"Aw, Chris, this is too sweet."

He motioned for me to have a seat which I did, and he sat next to me. "You like it?" he asked, handing me the bowl of popcorn.

I nodded my head yes, suddenly too bashful to look at him in his eyes. "So I planned it out. We chat it up here for an hour, walk to that lake not too far from your house, enjoy the scenery, and then walked a couple blocks to that Jamaican restaurant on Tillie Street."

I eyed him and said, "Oh, a date night, huh?"

He leaned in kissed my lips and said, "I am here to stay, Kyla, and with that, I have to make you forget about this Keith. So, yes, a date night." I nodded my head that I understood as he continued. "Plus, I have some poetry here I was writing earlier. I want your take on it."

I grew excited as I dipped my hand into the popcorn bowl and said, "Yes, please do." Like a kid in a candy store, my eyes lit up, and my ears tuned in to listen to Chris read his poetry, and as he read his work, he grew even sexier to me. I had to squeeze my thighs tight as my clitoris began to become engorged and throb. This man was definitely getting some cool points.

βββ

Looking Gloria over I said, "You don't look too good."

"You ever wonder how life would be if you had ended up with someone else? I'm having one of those moments."

"Not with Victor, Gloria. I thought you two were good." I reached out for her hand and squeezed it.

"He is never around. I know he isn't always at work when he says it is. To top that off, I'm still an associate at the firm."

I looked her over with so much concern. She and I had started off at the firm at the same time, but as my career flourished, hers stalled. I don't know why, but I never took the time to find out. I was busy making sure mine didn't stall.

"I need a change or something," Gloria continued. I sat there and listened to my friend vent. I started to wonder how in the world I missed her being so unhappy. This, in turn, made me think of my sister Brittany too. Back home in Texas, I wonder if she was happy with Michael. Just then, I knew I had to go home for another visit.

Brittany

I STOOD THERE in front of the mirror and stared at my reflection. From my chubby face to my swollen hands my body wasn't mine anymore. I was so uncomfortable in my own skin. My eyes were bloodshot red, and the fact that they were swollen from tears that wouldn't stop coming didn't help.

I knew I was a sucker. LeAnn's words kept replaying over and over in my head. *Our babies have the same father.* I refused to believe that Michael lied to me day in and day out, but as I always said, men will be men.

My thoughts were interrupted by the sound of my ring tone. Erykah Badu's soulful voice was now echoing throughout the restroom. I pressed TALK and said, "Yes!"

"Checking in on you." My mother Lorraine's voice came through the cell as more tears began to erupt. I felt the tightness in my throat as I attempted to reply as if nothing was wrong.

"Hey, Mama."

"I'm coming by today. Made some stew yesterday and I have too much left over. What time do you get off?"

"Come by around six." My voice was low and calm. My best way of hiding the pain in my voice.

"Baby, are you OK?" Mama's voice changed from cheery to concern. I could hear the sounds of the Clark Sisters gospel group in the background. She was in a good mood. I refused to help her day go wrong.

"Just tired, Mama. I'll see you at six, OK?" She replied reluctantly, but if I knew my Mama, she was planning to interrogate me once she saw me. I ended the call and turned on the faucet and threw water onto my face. I looked bad, and I couldn't help the fact that I couldn't make myself look better. *Fat and ugly.* I refused to look in the mirror once more as I walked out of the restroom.

I made my way back to my desk where my boss had left a load of files to put away, calls to make, and letters to type up. I loudly exhaled as I picked up the first initial folder when I heard, "Kyla!"

I sank into my seat and closed my eyes. "What?" I was used to Michael popping up at my job to check in on me. I halfway looked forward to it. But today wasn't the time. Today, I just wanted to hate him and call it a day.

I could sense him walking closer to me as he continued. "I know LeAnn came to see you."

I'm sure you do. That bitch is obviously loony and didn't hesitate to call you to let you know my world was officially fucked up. I opened my eyes to attempt to not let him see me hurt, "Yeah, she did. I'm at work. I don't want to talk about this here."

"OK, I can respect that." Michael took a seat in front of my desk and leaned in closer. He moved with such caution as if he was afraid I had a gun hidden behind my desk and was going to shoot him if he said the wrong thing. *Ooooh, a gun's just what I need. Blow his ass away.*

"Respect it and leave then."

"Brittany, do you think I'm going to just walk away when I know what is going on in your head?" Michael was sitting in front of me with the saddest expression I had ever seen on his face. It shocked me once I evaluated his demeanor. Something wasn't right. He actually seemed concerned, and the confusion was showing all over my face.

"You look concerned," I stated mockingly.

"Do not restart that again, Brittany. You know I care about you. You know I will never hurt you," Michael argued.

"Wrong. I don't know that." There was a pause. Our mouths were both shut at the same time, and our eyes were stuck on each other as if we were daring each other to blink first.

Michael leaned in closer to me, almost completely over my desk, and whispered, "It's not true."

I looked away, taking my attention to the view outside my window. I suddenly wished I was somewhere else. Somewhere besides sitting here listening to this load of crap. Crap! Crap! Crap!

I set my attention away from him and out the window as I said, "For a woman to say what she said to me, you had to have slept with her. Meaning, in the time I was begging you not to hurt me and struggling with the idea of carrying this child and trusting you, you were in bed with her. Now, this we know isn't a lie." I turned my head back and faced him. "Just like all the others, you lie too. You're no better."

He didn't say anything. His position was stuck leaned over my desk staring me down as if he was thinking of the right thing to say. Not the most honest thing, but the right thing. I was tired. I was broken. I no longer had any fight left within my own soul. "I'm done," I said to him as calmly as I could. I didn't want to argue. I didn't want to cry. I just wanted to file these folders, make these phone calls, and type up these letters.

I pointed toward the door. "You can let yourself out."

Chris

THE CLOCK ON the wall read nine P.M. Many hours after Kyla was supposed to be home from work I sat there waiting. This waiting game was nerve crippling as I wondered where she was. Then again, I asked myself those questions, knowing good and well that she didn't owe me an explanation. I was crippling a squat in her home, eating her food, using her lights, bathing in her water. *Shit, I need to move.*

The candles I had lit for the dinner I had cooked were just about burnt out. I had long ago shut off the auto play of music by jazz musician Najee. As I sat in a dimly lit quiet room my phone buzzed. My brother Dean's name flashed across the screen. I hadn't spoken to him since I had left Fort Worth. He knew I was here pursuing his first love, the woman that he was supposed to be with. And although we loved the same woman, I patiently waited for my moment for ten years. The waiting game was over. I pressed decline on my phone and took my attention back to the table.

I stood up as the last candle burnt out and grabbed my jacket. With Kyla's house key in tow I opened the door and locked it shut.

"Heading out?"

I turned at the sound of her voice and noticed her walking outside of her unit at the same time as I. "Yeah, change in plans. Going to see what eateries are in walking distance." She smiled. I noticed a deep dimple in her left cheek and quickly started to assess who she was. "And you are?"

"Oh, shoot, sorry." She extended her hand. "Krishell. I stay in Unit 9 as you can see." She pointed to the door behind her as I nodded my head OK. Turning on my heels she called out, "Try Nino's. It's a Jamaican cuisine spot. Everything in there is bad for you, so you know it's good," she laughed.

"Oh yeah, I might just do that because I haven't eaten. I was waiting on . . ." My voice trailed off.

She interrupted that awkward moment and said, "Look, I was going there. If you want to walk together, I don't mind. I just moved in this complex and haven't met anyone yet." She pointed toward the street. "Well, shall we? I'm pretty hungry."

Looking back toward Kyla's front door and then back to Krishell I fumbled with my hands, finally placing them in my pocket. *It's just getting something to eat.* "Ummm, sure, lead the way."

As I followed her onto the sidewalk the moonlight created a silhouette against the ash fault of her physique. I couldn't help but noticed the rise in her ass as it bounced back and forth. Her bronzed calves were extenuated in her red stilettos. I noticed I was giving her a head-to-toe assessment and jerked my eyes back upward.

Krishell turned around and jokingly said, "You can walk beside me, you know. I'm starting to think you're looking at something back there."

"Who me? Naw." I gave a nervous chuckle. She laughed as well and signaled for me to speed up, which I did.

βββ

Grabbing a beer I downed its contents to block the burning spices in my mouth as Krishell buckled over in laughter. "Oh, come on now, Chris, it isn't that spicy."

Taking the napkin to wipe my eyes I laughed out and said, "Woman, you must not have any taste buds. This shit is burning my mouth."

Krishell placed her hand over her heart as if she was innocent and said, "No, not I. I am but a victim of this here good Jamaican food. I could eat this stuff all day." She took a huge bite from her plate and hummed as she rubbed her belly.

I laughed out. "Oh, you got jokes, huh? So you can take it, but I can't." I knew the words were true but opted out of challenging her ability to eat this food without so much as a flinch or a need for water.

She waved her hands at me and said, "OK, OK, I have to admit it, I'm Jamaican, so this food is second nature to me."

I raised an eyebrow. "Jamaican?"

"My parents are full-blooded Jamaican, so that makes me Jamaican, but I was born here. Lived in D.C. all my life but moved into my new townhome, next to you, might I add, to be closer to my boutique. Traffic here is psychotic."

"Oh yeah. Tell me about it. I have only been here a couple of weeks, and I am not feeling the commute time here."

"Where did you relocate from?"

"Texas."

"Oh yeah? Hot there, huh?"

"Depends on the season but most say, yep, it's hot." Our conversation went on for what seemed like hours, and once I noticed it was well after midnight, I suddenly remembered it was supposed to be Kyla sitting across from me. Not Krishell.

Chance

"STILL MEAN AS hell, huh?"

Brittany turned around in the aisle we stood inside of the market and said, "Chance, don't start with me today."

I threw my hands up in surrender and said, "Here we go." I rushed up to her to reach the top shelf for the sauce she was aiming for. "Are you cooking tonight?"

"Why?" she blurted out.

I dropped the sauce in her grocery cart and proceeded to walk back to my cart. One thing Brittney had was a never-ending attitude. "Congrats on the baby," I called out as I pushed my cart away from her and walked on.

A long pause overtook our aisle and before I turned the corner I heard Brittney call out, "Thanks!" It was a softer tone now. One in which I knew she was trying to make peace. But when she wasn't talking that was when it was peaceful. Call me a fool but months without so much as a hello from her and this was our reunion conversation.

I turned my head around and just before I turned the corner and was out of sight I smiled toward her. I ended our exchange with a simple wink of an eye and off I went on my way.

I didn't bother to get the rest of the things I needed out of the store. I headed for the cashier and checked out. No, I literally checked out. My mind was in a daze. *She's pregnant.* Brittney had to have been one of the hardest women I ever had to break down. I literally had to prove my love to her each and every day. Until one day I stopped giving a fuck.

Until this very moment I didn't even know she was pregnant. With my thoughts clouding my better judgment, I paid for my groceries and walked out the door pulling out my phone in the process.

"Yo, you won't believe who I just saw."

My friend's voice came through the receiver as he asked, "Who?"

"Brittney, man. Did you hear about her being pregnant? She can't be any more than five, six months looks like to me. I don't know."

"Pregnant? Seriously?"

"Seriously, dog. She's pregnant," I announced again hopping in my car to hurriedly pull off before I caught a glimpse of Brittney leaving the store.

"Where are you now?"

"Man, I'm pulling out of the grocery store where I just saw her."

"Pulling off? Why are you doing that? Did you ask about the baby? I mean, six months, dog, that's when y'all were together."

"Don't say it, man. Don't even let that shit slip from your mouth. She ain't pregnant by me."

He started to laugh out, and I was not in a laughing mood. "Yo, Brandon, man, shit isn't funny."

"Turn your car around, man, and ask ole Brit Brat. I mean, y'all were together for what? Four years? Shit, ask her."

I pressed my foot harder on the gas and sped further away. "Hell, no," I yelled into the phone before I pressed the END button. *If Brittney was carrying my child, I didn't want to know it today.*

Brittney

YOU EVER FEEL like your world is about to come crashing down? Today was maybe my day. Here I was shopping and minding my own damn business when the past slapped me in my face. Chance Jamison. I had loved that man since college and before that, but things changed. And they changed quickly. Not too long after him came Michael, and here I am with the same type of man.

I pushed my basket to the side and walked away. I wasn't in the mood for cooking any more. I wasn't going over to Mama's house either. I just didn't feel like it. I still struggled with the idea that I wasn't following in my own mother in her footsteps. I was pregnant and unwedded.

Hopping in my car, I took a deep breath and immediately put my air on full blast. Putting it in reverse and speeding out of the parking lot I headed straight for Taco Bell.

I screamed my order to the speaker box, "Two bean burritos, a Double Decker, and a large Coke."

I ignored her repeating the order back to me and sped up to the window with my money dangling out of my car even before she had the chance to say hello. *Just give me my damn food.*

I was in Taco heaven when she handed me my food in exchange for the money. I didn't even wait to drive off before taking that first bite. This would relax my mind for just a moment anyhow.

βββ

I opened the door to my apartment and wobbled in. The lights were on, the TV was on. Damn, he was here.

"Get out!" I yelled. I could tell he was in the kitchen cooking something. Perfect, because I was ready to eat within the next hour.

He turned the corner with a water bottle in his hand. "Babe."

"Michael, is there something you need here? As a matter of fact, give me back my damn key. You don't need to come check on me. I'll be fine."

"I put some chicken in the stove for you." He bent down in front of me and proceeded to take my shoes off of my feet. I kicked my leg out, hitting him in his left shoulder. He fell backward onto his back and looked up to me. His expressions were first confusion, and then anger.

I folded my arms and dared him to do something. "Oh, you mad?"

He kneeled down and dropped his head in his hands, and as if nothing just happened, he scooted back over to me and began again to attempt to take off my shoes. When I reached backward to give another hard thrust with my leg he caught me in midair.

"Put your leg down." His voice was stern and damn near mean. It scared the hell out of me. His voice was always low, soft spoken, and he rarely if ever held an attitude toward me. I didn't know what to do with this reaction so I put my foot down.

"I am not going to fight you," he continued.

"Fight me for what? I didn't do anything. Now, you? Ha! That's a whole other story."

"What do you want me to do? Sit here and allow you to kick the shit out of me?" Michael yelled.

"Oh, you're yelling now. The real Michael is really starting to come out."

He stood up so quickly I nearly became dizzy as my eyes jolted up quickly to follow his movements. He walked over to my kitchen table and grabbed his car keys.

"That's what you do too."

With pure annoyance in his voice he said, "What, Brittney?"

"Walk away."

"Look, do you want me to walk away or stay? Which one do you want? I'm trying so damn hard to be here, Britt, but you make it hard. I swear."

Yelling at the top of my lungs, I said, "*I* make it hard? I am only with you now because you used to make me smile."

"I used to what?"

"Now all I see is an ever-changing Michael. Explain LeAnn," I blurted.

"Oh, so now you want to talk about her?"

I stood up and folded my arms above my huge belly and over my breasts. "I'm waiting."

"She's lying. Simple. What do I need to explain?"

I laughed to myself. Men could be so simpleminded. They think the shortest replies are always the best. They think the less they say then we will accept that and just shut our mouths. Wrong. I wasn't that type of chick. I wanted answers. My laughter escaped my mouth, and I didn't hide the fact that I felt his response was hilarious.

"You know what's funny, Michael?"

He blew out air and jerked his head toward me, clearly showing an attitude. I continued, "No woman can come to my house, look me in my face, and say she is carrying your child too. You see, this statement can only be said if you slept with her. And if you slept with her, it was when we were together. And you know what that sums up to be? Another lying-ass Negro."

He stared at me, our eyes locked in on one another. My heart was nearly sitting in my throat as pain, agony, and anger overcame my entire being. I wanted to cry. I wanted to scream. I wanted for my declaration to be wrong.

Michael opened his mouth slowly and said, "I can't argue with the woman I love, who is carrying our child, who I am trying so desperately to be with. And I always told you I will never lie to you. I will do my best to never hurt you. So I'm going to keep my promise." Walking up to me, Michael stood only a few inches away from my pregnant belly where our son was growing and said, "I did sleep with her."

In a split second, my hand was slamming down on his face cutting his skin like a knife. Oh yeah, I slapped him, and when I was done, I searched the room for something to hit him with.

Keith

I KNOCKED LIGHTLY on her office door before walking in. She looked up and smiled. I said, "Kyla, have you ever wondered why you are so damn beautiful?"

She pushed herself back from her desk and smiled while getting up to greet me. "Now, that, I can say, I honestly have." We laughed as we exchanged platonic kisses to the cheek. In the office we tried our best to keep things professional, but it was hard. She made it seem easy though, and I guess I couldn't argue with that. The less I did in public where Gloria could see, the better. Thinking that thought, just as I was about to ask Kyla a question I heard her voice.

"Hey, bestie." I blew out air in annoyance, realizing Gloria was here, before turning around and signaling with my eyes for Gloria to leave. Gloria ignored me and said, "Every time I come to see my friend, Keith, you are just magically here." Her narcissistic tone drilled into my last nerve as I tried to ease my breathing that suddenly began to race with aggravation.

"I wonder why?" I sarcastically replied. I started to dissect her game. When I came near Kyla, Gloria suddenly popped up. Now, I wasn't a fool. I was quite educated, having graduated from Columbia University. I knew very well that Gloria made herself available so that I was never alone with Kyla. I would have to put a stop to this. I began to put together my game plan when I heard Gloria speak.

"How about we all go hang out tonight? Isn't your friend still in town?" Gloria quizzed Kyla.

I raised an eyebrow. *Friend?* "Who are you talking about?" Kyla's facial expression toward Gloria could have sliced her face in half if it were a knife.

"A friend from Fort Worth is here. He's relocating, and, no, I think he's busy tonight." Kyla quickly walked back to her desk and sat down, placing all of her focus onto her computer. "By the way, I do have this pitch I need to finish today, so I'll be busy tonight too."

I walked over to Kyla and said, "I'll call you later on." Walking out, I turned my head to look at Gloria and sternly said, "Gloria!"

She rolled her eyes and stared at me without as much as a blink. "Keith!"

Kyla looked up from her desk and called out, "What is this, a stare-down?"

I marched out of her office before I managed to incriminate myself any further. It was official. I had to get rid of Gloria in the worst way before her behavior became more than just a stare-down.

Brittney

THE PHONE RANG twice, then the person hung up. This damn stupid bitch. I struggled turning over onto my left side again to rest. My mind was clouded. I was tired, and I felt fatter than a fat kid on a hot summer day. When I heard a knock on my door I sat up straight in the middle of my bed as quickly as I could. By the size of my belly, it wasn't that quick. I looked at my clock. It was only ten after nine at night.

I scooted out of the bed and reached for my bat behind my bedroom door. I didn't call out to the door as I didn't want whoever it was to know I was near it. I tiptoed all the way there and looked out the peephole. Then I raised an eyebrow and immediately became confused.

Unlocking the locks on my door I kept the bat by my side as I opened the door and tilted my head to the side giving him a head-to-toe assessment. "Ummm, yeah?"

"It's late. Going to let me in?"

"Chance, what the hell are you doing just showing up at my door like a damn thief in the night?"

He walked past me and didn't answer as he beelined it to my kitchen with groceries in his hands.

"I know your big ass is hungry. So I brought you some of your favorite stuff." He laughed as he started to put the food up.

I slammed my door and placed on my Oscar-winning performance of the biggest and baddest attitude.

"Don't go there with the ritual, Britt. You know you want me to put up this food. As a matter of fact, are you hungry now?"

I paused in midstride as it hit me as soon as he asked. I could use something to eat. "Yeah, go on ahead and cook me something then, Mr. Nice Guy." I plopped down on my sofa and smirked. He walked over and stood in the walkway of my kitchen. I turned my attention back to the TV. *Chance.* My first love, one of the few men I have ever loved. And not even a full year after our breakup, there he was standing right in front of me. When I started to think of the reason we broke up, he interrupted my thoughts.

"Fish tacos it is," he announced. I would be lying if I said I didn't immediately start to salivate at the mouth with the announcement of him cooking his famous fish tacos I used to beg him to cook.

"Fine!" I pretended to act unnerved as I secretly was doing a dance in my head.

When I heard my phone ring I rose up to speed walk back to my room. Clicking TALK I said, "Hey, Tionna, what's up, girl?"

"Oh, you sound awfully cheery. What's going on with you?"

"Oh well, you know how I get when I get a good nap in. What's up?" I lied.

"I was calling to check up on you. Do you need anything?"

"No, ma'am, I'm good. Going to lie around and watch TV. But call me tomorrow." I hurriedly rushed her off of the phone as I heard Chance make footsteps back to my room. I ended the call without Tionna so much as saying good-bye.

Leaning his body up again my door frame I examined him again. In the five years I have known him, he stood just over 5'9, was darker than the black cherry itself, slim but stocky in all the right places, had big feet, big hands, big—well, you know . . . Everything was right on him. He wore his hair low and curly now with a grown man's gold-T. His heavy tone called to me, bringing me out of a hypnosis that was caused by his good looks.

"That was Tionna." He was telling me versus asking me. I didn't reply. He lowered his head. I could tell he was digesting the fact that I was still friends with Tionna. He leaned back up to turn to walk away. "Come on, you can help me wash off the fish."

I followed him as if I was a kid being chastised. I didn't want to talk about my friendship with Tionna. I didn't want to discuss the obvious fact that I was pregnant. And I didn't want to hint that I had missed him. Mainly because now I was carrying another man's child.

Michael

I KNOCKED ON her door again and no answer. I stood there five minutes before finally pulling out my key and unlocking the door myself. I walked in to smell the after aroma of fried fish. The TV was off, and so were all the lights. She wasn't here. It was ten in the morning, and Brittany wasn't at home, work, or answering her phone.

We had a doctor's appointment today, and it was set to be at eleven. I walked in and out of rooms in her apartment noticing that she had left not too long ago. I could still feel the steam of the shower that she had taken throughout her bedroom where the bathroom door was open. I smelled the aroma of her perfume.

Turning on my heels I rushed out the door and onto the highway. If she had gone to the appointment without me she was taking this being mad at me a little too far. It wasn't even twenty minutes before I was pulling up in front of the doctor's office.

Once inside, I noticed she wasn't seated. I went to the receptionist to ask if she had checked in. She hadn't. So I found a seat and pulled out my cell phone. I texted her. No reply.

I tried to hide the obvious annoyance on my face as I sat back rubbing my sweaty palms over my Calvin Klein suit pants. Aggravated, I pulled off the matching jacket and draped it across my right leg. Distractedly, I picked up a nearby magazine and began to roam through the pages until I looked up and saw Brittany walk through the door.

Throwing the magazine in the seat next to me I stood up but noticed she wasn't dressed in her work clothes or one of the maxi dresses I had bought her. For weeks now she had complained about her size so I went and bought her some dresses that swayed all the way down to her ankles. She loved them. But today, she had on a sundress with a bow that tied across her waist, bringing more attention to her growing belly. She wore golden sandals and purple bucket hair that fell just over her shoulders. Her hair was down underneath. She had on makeup. The perfect blend of makeup, at that. I tilted my head to the side. She looked happy, calm, beautiful.

I smiled, walked over to her, extended my arms, and said, "Brittany!" My tone was soft enough to woo a sleeping a baby. Placing my hands on the small of her back, she surprisingly looked toward me as I leaned down and kissed her cheek. "Babe, you look beautiful today."

Turning her head slighting away, her eyes bulged out of her sockets as her mouth dropped. It wasn't the reaction I was seeking. Seeing her reaction, I squinted my eyes in confusion.

"I didn't know you would be here. I . . . I hadn't talked to you."

"I just texted you, and, of course, I would be here. Do I ever miss any appointments?" I replied.

Placing her hand on my chest she pushed me backward gently away from the door she just walked in and said, "I am here with someone. I mean, not someone—just a friend, so don't make something out of it that it isn't."

What? Looking over her shoulder I saw this big-ass hat that now was the most annoying thing to be tapping at my last nerve at this moment. Then I noticed a dark male walk through. The complete opposite to my shade but definitely wasn't ugly as I was curious to see. *He* was with Brittany? But why?

"Who is that?" I gave him a head-to-toe scrutiny as he noticed Brittany, smiled, and walked over. I didn't like his smile. I didn't like the way he was looking at my woman.

Brittany followed my eyes to see who I was looking at and said, "That's him. A friend from college."

"Men and women can't be friends," I quickly said before he was too close to hear. I moved around Brittany and cut his stride in half. He finally noticed me for the first time since entering and tilted his head with curiosity as I extended my hand.

"Williams. Michael Williams. I am Brittany's boyfriend."

His smile was halfway gone and instantly was replaced with a look of confusion. Then as if the dots connected, he took my hand in his and said, "Oh, the baby daddy." He said it with a tone that annoyed the hell out of me. As if he was downplaying my role in Brittany's life. I was more than a baby daddy, more than a sperm donor, more than just a friend. Hell, I was the role that was most important. She was my woman, and that was my child.

"No, her 'family' sounds a little better. What's up? Y'all reconnecting or something?" I interjected.

Brittany wobbled in between us and said, "Chance, I'm good now. Michael will drive me home. But thanks for yesterday and this morning. I'll call you." She leaned in and hugged him. I looked away as the anger I felt was beginning to seep through my pores. *She is fucking with me, right? I KNOW I'm not tripping.*

Chance hugged her back, gave me a head nod, and walked away. "What kind of name is Chance?" I asked Brittany as he walked out the door.

Instead of answering me she walked over to the receptionist and checked in. This day just got a little more interesting as I remembered Brittany tell Chance "thank you for yesterday and this morning." Yeah, she *was* fucking with me all right if she thought I was going to let that comment go.

Chris

I TOOK ANOTHER swallow of my beer as Keith and his friend, James, kept talking about the Washington Wizards game. I wasn't a fan of the team, but when Keith invited me to the game I agreed. As they say, keep your friends close and your enemies closer. Did Kyla know? She would tonight as soon as I got home. I smirked listening to Keith give his philosophy of the game.

I secretly wished for him to shut the hell up. Everything that came out of his mouth was annoying. And to be honest, I wasn't so sure how long I was going to keep my being with Kyla a secret. I mean, what man does that? Here I was, coming clear across the country out on what seemed like a fucking date with my girl's man.

I dropped my head in embarrassment as if the entire stadium knew that I was being soft in this situation. "I'm a

Mavericks' fan, to be honest," I interjected, cutting off Keith and James's conversation.

"Oh yeah, you're from Texas, right?" James asked. I nodded my head yes. He began to talk about how some of our starting players were some of the best in the league. I nodded my head arrogantly and said, "Yep, this I know." I was bored with this wizard's game.

Keith asked, "How do you like it in D.C. so far?"

"It's cool, dating a woman here already," I said nonchalantly.

They both laughed, "Oh yeah, it's easy to find women here in D.C. There's plenty of them. Keith here, my man, can tell you that. I'm married; I try to be good," James added.

Keith waved off his hand and eyed James who immediately got the hint to stop while he was ahead.

"Oh, so there's more than just Kyla?" I quizzed. Men didn't ask these questions. Men didn't talk about these things; it went unsaid that it was an unwritten rule to just stay in your own lane. But this situation was different; Kyla was the love of my life. If I could get him to walk away, then I could finally have her focused on us and our future.

Keith took a swallow of his beer and turned his body toward me. "And if there were?"

His demeanor was a challenge, as if he was daring me to even ask him these questions. I laughed a little. Not that what he said was funny but how he was reacting to my question. Dude was a piece of work. I would care less who the hell he was fucking if it wasn't Kyla. I picked up my beer, never taking my eyes off of him, and said, "I don't give a fuck if there was. Not about you, that is. But Kyla, that's a whole other story." Now *my* tone was a challenge. Daring him to say something else slick out of his mouth.

"Yo, fellas, am I missing something?" James asked.

"Apparently someone holds some animosity. You all right, dude? You all swollen in the chest," Keith arrogantly added.

I smirked and eyed him. "I don't know you that well, my dude, but perhaps we should ask Gloria!" My accusatory tone was deep and heavy as I waited for his reply. His arrogant smirk was replaced with an uncomfortable frown.

"Gloria?"

"Sure, why not?" I added.

"Let's just pay attention to the game and y'all get into this another time," James suggested, trying to defuse the situation. But it wasn't going to work. At this very moment, Keith and I eyed each other, daring to look away as if there were no one else in the stadium.

Downing the remains of my drink I stood up and said replying to James, "Yeah, we can do that, and I'll be around."

Keith's eyes followed me with pure fire shooting from his pupils as I walked away. I knew I had opened up the door for nothing but trouble; then again, what led me to Kyla's heart was well worth it. This game went south quicker than I had planned. I guess I wasn't able to hold my tongue on the situation anyway. This shit was messier than a trick on *The Maury Show* not knowing who her baby daddy is. I would patiently wait to see what Keith's next move would be.

Kyla

MY FEET WERE pounding on the pavement as I raised my hand to block the sun's beams while dodging other runners as I made way around the track. I could feel the burning in my chest as I fed more fuel into each step that I took. I hadn't run in weeks, and I could tell that I was out of shape.

"All work and no training," Gloria yelled out from behind me.

I slowed down so that she could catch up, and not to lie, I was plain tired. I breathed in and out of my mouth heavy as I tried to catch my breath. "I'm exhausted. Let's just walk."

Gloria laughed when she finally reached me. "I don't blame you. I'm already craving some jerk chicken from Papi's."

I rolled my eyes and laughed. "How are you thinking of food right now?" I clutched my side to lessen the pain of an arriving cramp. "This is ridiculous how tired I am."

"Yep, sure is." Gloria's teasing voice burst into laughter. In an effort to come back with a smart remark I watched Gloria's eyes trail to a woman behind me. Her laughed stopped in midair. I jerked around to see a familiar face.

"Nadine, hey, what are you doing here?"

Nadine walked over to me and gave me a causal hug and looked at Gloria. "Hey, lady," she said to me. "Hi, I'm Nadine." She extended her hand to Gloria. I watched Gloria freeze in place as she didn't blink or speak as Nadine spoke out.

"Oh, I'm sorry. Yeah, nice to meet you." Gloria took her hand, and then quickly dropped it.

Shrugging my shoulders I turned back to Nadine and said, "What are you doing here? You quit the Zumba class too?" I laughed.

Laughing as well, Nadine replied, "Girl, please, that instructor was psycho. Of course I quit. After you told me about this runners' park I had to check it out. So you and your friend run here often, huh?"

"I'm getting back into the swing of things."

"Well, let's do lunch this week or something, cool?"

I hugged her back and agreed. As she ran away I turned on my heels to tell Gloria to come on. But when I turned around she wasn't there.

I called out her name and looked all around me to see if she just ran off, but I didn't see her anywhere. Tilting my head and totally confused, I pulled out my cell phone and texted her.

GLORIA, WHERE DID YOU GO?

After a couple of minutes of no reply I slowly walked back to my car still searching around the park. *Weird,* I thought. I stood there puzzled. I rewound her disappearing act, and it dawned on me just then that the moment she saw Nadine she was stuck in place. Now what the hell was I missing? Apparently, something else was going down that I didn't know about.

This surely must be a small world.

Brittany

I LOOKED AT my phone and nothing. Not so much as a text from Michael. He dropped me off at home yesterday with not one word, a kiss, a good-bye. Nothing. Now today, still nothing. I shouldn't be mad, though. I didn't do anything. OK, so yeah, Chance came over, cooked for me, cleaned up a little, and we watched movies that whole night. So yeah, I spent almost 24 hours with him. I know that's wrong, but we still had a LeAnn situation.

The conversation still hadn't been made and obviously it was about that time. So I texted Michael. I must have stared at my phone for two hours, and he never replied. I rolled out of my bed finally, annoyed and bored, and looked for something to put on. I brushed my hair up into a bun, placed on some makeup to look the best I possibly could, and slipped on my sandals.

I called Tionna on my way out.

"Hey," she said.

"Can you meet me at the Lyrical Lounge? I'm bored as hell and need to get out."

"Yeah, I'm not too far from there. Are you OK? Need me to bring you something?"

"Nope, just your company. I'll see you in a bit." I hung and hopped in my car, headed straight to the lounge for some R&R.

βββ

The lounge was halfway filled, which was just perfect for me. I didn't too much want to be seen by a lot of people anyway. The host sat me at a table near the rear as a local jazz band was playing. I looked at the appetizer menu and order some potato skins to start off with.

"Brit Brat, what are you doing here?"

I looked up and laughed out. "What the hell? Chance! Why the hell are you popping up everywhere?"

Taking a seat across from me he said, "I manage this spot now. I thought I told you that."

"You told me a spot, but not this one. This is my favorite spot. Now I got to find somewhere else to go." I poked my lip out.

"Come on, now, Brit, you ain't got to act like you all mad at a brother. Let me get you a strawberry daiquiri. Virgin, that is. On the house."

"OK, don't get fired getting me free drinks. I ain't liable," I called out after him as he walked off to the bar.

He waved his hand off as I slouched in my seat to get more comfortable. I eyed Chance walking around the room and admired the man that he was. Tall, dark, handsome, and apparently sweet. *Why did I break up with him?*

I shook my head trying to knock those thoughts out of it as I noticed Chance walking back to me with my potato skins and daiquiri. "For you, madam!" He placed the items in front of me.

I smiled and thanked him as he sat down in front of me again.

"How was yesterday at the doctor's office?"

"It was good. The baby is healthy, big, and I am perfectly fine." I bit into my food. He smiled and nodded his head. I looked him over and with my eyes I tried to dissect his motives, as if I had laser-eye vision and could see through him. But I couldn't.

Chance laughed and said, "What, Brittany? What are you trying to figure out?"

"Oh, nothing. I mean, you just seem . . ."

"Nice." He tugged at his collar and pretended to dust his shoulders. "That's because I am."

I laughed and rolled my eyes. "Whatever."

"Well, well, well, isn't this interesting." I heard Tionna's voice and my food dropped out of my hand in shock. I had totally forgotten that she was meeting me here.

Chance's smile turned into a look of disgust. "I need better security for this place." He began to rub his hands together and cracked his knuckles. I remember him doing that when he was angry or agitated.

"Tionna, hey." I looked up and looked her over. Her weight was switch to one leg as she popped the gum in her mouth annoyingly. She was upset too.

I heard Chance whisper something underneath his breath as he rose up. "Brittany, I'll leave you alone with this."

Tionna jerked her head and turned to Chance. "What the fuck do you mean *this*? You better respect me, Chance. What the hell are you doing here anyway?"

Chance stepped toward her in a matter of seconds. His fist still balled in his one hand as he grazed his knuckles. If Tionna were a man, I would bet that he was one second from punching her out. I sat there eyes bulged and nearly begging them with my childlike tone to not cause a scene.

"I manage this lounge, and I can control just about anyone who can come in here. So I suggest you watch your tone with me." Chance threw up his hands and added, "Why the fuck is she still in your life, Brittany, if I am not?"

I opened my mouth to speak, but Tionna interjected and said, "Negro, please. It's always been bitches over you trifling Negroes." I dropped my head into my hand as Tionna displayed the first evidence of a female about to get really loud. I didn't want any embarrassment or for Chance to be arguing with her at his place of business.

"Chance, Tionna, please just walk away," I begged.

"No, I'm good. I'll catch you later, Brittany, and then you can tell me when this all even started up again. This is some straight bull," Tionna yelled as she turned on her heels and walked away.

I looked up at Chance who was still standing in place watching Tionna walk out of the lounge. I called out to him, but it was as if he was in a daze. He didn't flinch, and it looked like he was even holding his breath.

"I just saw the woman who took you away from me for the first time, and all I kept imagining were my hands around her neck."

"Can you get me a to-go box? I'm ready to go."

"Yeah, walk with me outside. I got to talk to you."

After packing up my food I followed Chance to his car and sat in the passenger seat. I wasn't prepared for what he was about to tell me. Then again, it's been a year, and this conversation was long overdue.

Chance

SITTING IN THE driver's seat of my car I looked at Brittany who had now opened up her to-go box and was eating her food, and I asked, "Want to drive to the French Lake?"

"Sure, that would be cool. I haven't been there in forever."

The drive was quiet. The only sound was classic RNB from 105.7 through the radio system. In fifteen minutes, I was pulling up the lake and hopping out. I walked around and opened Brittany's door as she took her time getting out.

"I can't do too much walking now," she joked.

"Walking is good for you and the baby." I extended my hand, and she took it.

She blew out hot air in annoyance of my declaration and followed me onto the sidewalk. The sun was now setting and was beaming in the center of the lake, creating perfect scenery for this moment. "You got me here," Brittany announced.

"We used to walk here sometimes during those weekends from college, remember that?"

She nodded her head yes. "Yep, it was our spot." She looked around and took a deep breath of the fresh air. "Haven't walked here in ages."

"I come about once a week. I run the track at least twice to work out a little."

"Oh yeah?" she added.

We grew quiet for what seemed like an eternity, both of us lost in our own thoughts as we made our way around the lake.

"Why is Tionna still around? That woman is evil."

"I don't know her to be evil, Chance. She's been my girl since high school. Other than Mama, she's there for me."

"I know this, Brit. Imagine why I was lost when she made it her mission to break us up. The bitch is evil."

Brittany stopped in her footsteps and said, "Really, we are calling her bitches now?"

"She better be glad I'm not calling her more than that. Get rid of her like you did me. You got rid of the wrong person."

"I believed her; that's it."

I stuffed my hands in my pockets and kicked a rock that was in my path. "I never tried to fuck that girl. Tionna was a lying-ass jealous female, Brittany. Even a year later, I am telling you the truth. I ain't do nothing with that girl."

"Tell me again," Brittany said. "Besides, it doesn't matter anyway. Look at me."

I raised an eyebrow as I stopped her and placed both of my hands on her shoulders. "I have never tried to do anything with Tionna. Did I fuck up sometimes back then? Yes. I was young, Brittany. But I have grown in this past year. And not having you in my life made me realize that. Do you know how hard it was to be with someone nearly every day of my life for four years, and then suddenly, they're gone?"

Brittany forced my hands off of her shoulders as I could tell she was getting emotional. "It doesn't matter anyway."

"I know you keep saying that because you're pregnant."

Sarcastically she replied, "Ugh, you think? I'm with someone else now too, Chance. I'm having a baby with someone else less than a month after even knowing him. I fucked up, I know, but we were done. We are done, and there is no going back."

I looked away from her as I saw her eyes swell with tears.

"Do you believe me when I say I didn't try anything with Tionna? She lied to you, Brittany."

"If she lied, why? Why would she lie on you, Chance?"

"Ask *her*, Brittany, because for a year I've been trying to figure that out." Turning to her I continued, "You think I'm not hurting over the fact that your so-called best friend made it her mission to break us up, accomplished that goal, and when I finally see you again, you're pregnant?"

"I don't know," she mumbled.

"Only seven months ago, Brittany, we had slipped up and I was in your bed. Are you seven months pregnant, Brittany? Tell me, is that my baby?" The question I had wanted to ask since I saw her in the grocery store a couple weeks back had finally slipped out.

Brittany dropped her head and stared at her growing belly. The wind was my only answer now as I watched her watch her belly. A growing child was there. A child I was hoping she would say was mine. If that was my child I would finally make things right between us. Get rid of Tionna's evil ass and finally be back with Brittany.

"You made me bitter, you made me hate all men, and you made me vulnerable. Honestly, is this your baby? Your guess is as accurate as mine." She looked up and stared me in the eyes. "I'm sure, though, this is Michael's baby. The time stamp doesn't lie. I was with you a month before I was with him. He's it." She cried. "I do love you, Chance, but what's done is done."

I didn't shy from the fact that tears were now streaming down my face. "It doesn't matter, Brittany, because I walked away and gave up on you believing in me a year ago. I won't walk away now."

Michael

OUTSIDE OF MY office I looked up and noticed LeAnn leaned up against my car. I rolled my eyes and blew out hot air. "Crazy ass, what the hell are you doing here, LeAnn? You already are fucking up shit with my woman. Now, are you trying to add stalker to your résumé?"

I elbowed her arm to move her from in front of my front door to open it when she said, "We are having a girl. Aren't you excited?"

I rolled my eyes and looked at her. I grunted hard as if I was trying to clear an object stuck in my throat and started to run the right words in my head to say to her. *This is your place of business, and this chick is psycho. Get in your car and just drive away.*

"Excuse me, but I have somewhere to be." I jerked open my door as she called out that I would see her soon. I pulled out my cell phone as I placed my car in reverse, halfway wanting LeAnn to be behind it so I could run her ass over. I shook my head and cursed underneath my breath. I knew I had to get a hold of this if I was hoping to run over a pregnant lady.

I dialed my brother Omar's number. He picked up on the third ring. "Yo, bro, call your lawyer at Brown and Davis. I got to get a restraining order on this chick and a paternity test."

"Brittany?"

"Hell, no, man. LeAnn's crazy ass. She is showing up at my job now."

"How did she know where you work?"

"Crazy females have a way. Let's get this handled quick. I got to get things ironed out with Brittany. So call me with the meeting date with the lawyer."

"OK, bro, I'm on it."

I hung up and made my way to Brittany's house. I had purposely not called her all day. Now, going on seven o'clock, I knew I couldn't go a whole day without talking to her. I needed to make things right.

βββ

Poking her head out of the door, she gives me nothing but attitude. "What?"

I smiled at her. I had to admit I liked the fact that she was feisty, sure of herself, and was a true-shit talker. She was tuff. It was one thing that I loved—and hated—about her at the same time. "Come on, babe, let me in." She was stuck in place as I only saw her head poked out.

"You know you should call before you just pop over."

"Since when do I have to do that?" I dropped my hands to my sides as the seriousness in her tone wasn't so funny anymore. I leaned forward against her door and whispered, "I brought you some chicken. And it's fried."

She looked down at my hands and eyed the William's Chicken bag and smirked. "Ugh. You know I can't turn that down. Fine, bring your ass in." She moved back, opening the door all the way as I laughed.

I plopped down on the sofa and patted a spot next to me for her to join me. She purposely sat across from me on the other couch and extended her hands. "Chicken, please."

I sat up and placed it on the table in front of her as she began to dig in. "How was your day today?" I asked.

"Fine." She had already taken her first bite.

"Sorry I didn't call all day. Actually had to work this weekend. Just got off and came here." She didn't reply; she just nodded her head OK. "Are you mad at me? I know yesterday was pretty interesting for us both." She just eyed me with the expression that read, "Shut up!"

"I'm fine, Michael," she said in between bites.

"Are you ready to talk now?"

"Talk about what?"

"LeAnn, Brittany. Let's talk about what we both want to know."

She stubbornly rolled her eyes and said, "I'm cool. I don't actually care."

I chuckled a little for her to hear me. "That's a lie. Since you insist on being stubborn, I'll just tell you what you need to know."

Brittany pushed herself back into the couch, curling her feet under her legs. "Talk!"

Suddenly the room fell quiet. I reached for the TV remote and shut it off. I knew that the nervousness I was experiencing was clearly showing on my face. I didn't want to have this conversation, but it had to be said. Once we were done, I definitely had some questions for her.

"Let's keep it real, Brittany; I was doomed to win your heart from the jump. You consistently always pushed me away."

"Is this how you want to start the conversation?" Brittany interjected, causing me to lose my train of thought. I threw my hand up to signal for her to not talk. Surprisingly, she just stopped talking when I asked.

I continued, "I fucked up, OK? I'm not going to sit here and say that this was totally on me either. Because what's done is done. LeAnn coming to you was completely a mind game for her. I have honestly tried to deal with her since she started harassing me, but once she found out about you, I knew it was only a matter of time before you knew about her."

"Go on, Michael, get to the part I want to know," Brittany yelled.

"Yes, I did have sex with her, Brittany, but it was after we broke up. After you pushed me away and told me to leave, after you walked away from me. I didn't go out and seek this woman. It just happened."

"Oh, so you getting her pregnant is *my* fault?"

I threw up my hand again. "First off, I had sex with her only once and with a condom. I never dated her, barely knew her, and she is like six months pregnant. We slept together like four months ago."

Brittany raised an eyebrow. "Four months ago, and she is six months? Why would she be coming after you then, Michael, if these dates are true?"

"She's crazy. I keep telling you this. Believe me for once, OK? I will not beg you to carry our child just to deceive you. I wouldn't be trying to buy you a house to do you wrong. I wouldn't be standing right here trying to be with you, wanting to love you, and for us to be a family if I was lying. I don't need to lie, Brittany."

Brittany dropped her head in her hands and began to cry out. "This is déjà vu," she screamed. She became so hysterical that I rushed over to her on my knees and began to hold her.

"Brittany, what's wrong? Baby, talk to me," I asked her over and over again, confused at her hysterical breakdown.

I jerked up in defense mode when I heard a man from behind me say, "She's crying because of me." I turned around to see Chance standing in the living room. I looked at him and back at Brittany, and then back to him again.

Raising an eyebrow with my fists balled into knots I sternly said, "Am I *missing* something here?"

Chance

LIFE DOESN'T HAVE to sit here in your face and laugh its ass off. But life was laughing its ass off right about now. It was laughing so hard that I could hear the echoes of its laughter in the dead air. In every step that I took, I could feel the earth giggling beneath me and mocking me of the mistakes I have made. This situation was no better. In a matter of days, the love I have tried to get rid of for a year was back as if it had never left. I was in love with Brittany. I was in love with a woman who would give birth to another man's child in three months. I had three months before she would no longer just be Brittany.

I watched Michael look at me as if he wanted to take away my life. He was confused as to why I was standing in Brittany's living room. But when he had showed up unannounced I had agreed to hide in Brittany's room to not cause any problems between them. I mean, anything to not stress her out.

We hadn't done anything. We were just here enjoying each other's company. Honestly, I don't know what I was doing. I knew I was wrong to complicate things for her. She was with him; she was carrying his child. But I couldn't help the fact that I was here first. That the spot Michael was standing in *I* stood in a year ago.

He was begging Brittany to believe him as I had done. But she didn't believe me. Instead, she walked away from me. Walked away from our history and didn't even look back. Brittany was always known to be tuff, mean, and guarded, but at that moment, I wanted her to show some type of humility about our situation. It was as if she didn't care to walk away from me.

She had moved on and discovering her carrying another man's child was stabbing at my heart every time I thought about it. This was some crazy mess to me. I was confused as to why this was my fate. I didn't understand why I lost the woman I had loved all those years to a lie only to witness another man beg for her love as I had done. Yeah, life was laughing its ass off at me. The joke was on me. I just knew I was being punked right now.

"Am I missing something?" Michael repeated.

"I stood where you were only a year ago asking Brittany to do the same thing. To forgive me," I replied.

Michael rushed up to me as Brittany suddenly had more than enough energy to hop off of the couch at the sight of Michael's sudden movements. "No. What I am asking you, what the hell are you doing here?"

Michael jerked his head around and began to look at Brittany up and down. His expression was confusion, anger, and hurt at the same time. "Who the fuck is this, Brittany, and why the hell do I keep seeing him around? Y'all together and shit alone in this house and the other day. What the hell am I missing? Play me for a fool?"

He was angry. I couldn't blame him. But his tone to Brittany was tapping at the last restraint I had in my body to not strike back.

"Look; nothing is going on. I was just—"

"What? Here? Again? Yeah, you two must think I'm the dumbest nigga on the planet." He looked back at Brittany and continued, "So this is why you kept pushing me away? For this nigga Chance?"

I stepped to Michael and said, "I'm going to need you to lower your tone when you are talking to her."

Brittany yelled out, "No, OK? Please y'all, just break it up."

I threw my hand toward her to step back. I didn't want her near us if I had to swing on him, which I was set to do at any second.

Michael laughed. Not that anything was funny, but he looked at Brittany as if she were disgusting, and then back at me as if I were the shit on the bottom of his shoe. "That kid ain't mine, is it?" he yelled out.

Brittany's surprised look pulled at my heart. Her eyes were filled with hurt, shock, and confusion. "Why would you say that?" she asked him.

"I've been trying to figure out you not coming down on me about LeAnn. You haven't pressured me to find out if I did get her pregnant; you have this nonchalant way about how you act toward me. It's like you don't give a fuck. It's starting to all make sense now. That ain't my kid anyway."

Brittany threw her head back in frustration. "Look, this conversation isn't going the way it should. Michael, this is *your* baby. I haven't done anything with Chance. It's just that—" Before Brittany could finish her sentence Michael had stepped around me and was walking toward the door. Brittany yelled after him, but he didn't stop or turn around. I rushed over to her and held her tight as she whelped in my arms.

I loved her, but I was starting to realize that my being around her was making her unhappy.

Kyla

I KNOCKED AGAIN on her door, and there I stood waiting. I began to tap my right foot in anticipation of her finally opening this door so I could see what was really going on. But still nothing. I decided to be stubborn and not move a muscle. Oh, she was going to come out, or I was going to come in.

"I'm not going anywhere, Gloria!"

I could hear the patting of her foot going back and forth, and then a thud. I jumped at the sound of the crashing object and began to knock hysterically on the door this time. Suddenly it swung open and a shirtless man came barging out.

Rushing backward to not touch him, the fear that was now rushing over my flesh was going into full gear. "Excuse me!" I screamed out.

His angry demeanor was threatening. His chest heaved in and out with his fist balled to his side. I had no idea who he was. I started to look him over. He was tall, at least 5 foot 11, heavy in his waist area; a black man with short, scruffy-looking hair that was matted at the roots. He didn't look too clean if you ask me.

"Bitch, you are interrupting my hour. Come the fuck back!" My mouth dropped open in fear, and my eyes bulged clear out of my sockets as I yelled out asking him who he was. He didn't answer. I backed away even more and began to move to dodge him in case he charged.

"Gloria!" I yelled out.

In an instant as I was about to turn on my heels to pull out my cell phone to call the cops I heard her voice. Low, soft, shaky, and as if this man wasn't about to charge toward me.

"Hey, Kyla, what's up, girl? Give me a second."

I stopped in my tracks, looked at the man, and then leaned my body to the right to look around him. I could feel tears swelling in my eyes before I could manage to speak. "Gloria!" I whispered.

Only yesterday she had disappeared on me from the park after we ran into Nadine. Since that very moment I had been trying to get in touch with her, and now, I stood here looking at her as if she were a strung-out crackhead. Her clothes disheveled, her eyes bloodshot red, her normal coffee-colored skin that complimented her Latino roots was now pale and nearly ghostlike.

She began to hug herself, rubbing her arms and shoulders as if she were cold. But the ninety-degree heat told a different story. It wasn't cold; it was as hot as hell, so why was she shaking and rubbing herself like that?

"Are you OK? What's going on?" My phone was in my hand as the man turned from Gloria, and then back to me.

"Strung-out bitch," he spat. He turned on his heels and rushed past Gloria, knocking her over hitting her shoulder. I rushed to help her up from the fall. She smelled. I scrunched my nose in disgust as I felt I was holding a bag of stinky garbage. Her hair was matted and sweated out. Her skin was damp and sticky.

When I opened my mouth to tell her just that, the man walked back toward us and stepped over our bodies to make his exit out of her home. "Tell Nadine I want my money back."

I jerked my head at the sound of Nadine's name and turned back to Gloria. I could tell the man had walked off, then I heard him get in a car and drive away. My eyes met Gloria's who was staring at me. Her eyes were pleading, her body limp, and as she dropped her head into my bosom, she whispered, "Now I know I'm in trouble."

The tears I was crying were burning and blocking my vision as I struggled to get up and pull Gloria up with me. I was confused. I was angry. I was afraid. I pulled out my phone and called the only person I knew could help me without asking too many questions. This just wasn't making any sense to me.

Chris

I RUBBED KYLA'S shoulder and asked her if she was OK. In truth, she was an emotional wreck. After bathing and clothing Gloria, we brought her back to sleep it off at Kyla's house. "Where is her husband Victor?"

I didn't know Victor; never have seen him since I had been here, but now the mystery of me not seeing him was becoming clearer to me. He must have left her. Coming from Fort Worth, there were those neighborhoods where it was common for you to see a drug addict walking down the streets. I didn't know if Gloria was on drugs, but from what I grew up seeing and from what I saw today, I wondered.

Kyla sat there quietly. I rubbed the back of neck and kissed her on her cheek. "I'm going to make everyone something to eat."

I walked into the kitchen and pulled out the ingredients to the jerk chicken pasta Krishell had told me about. I had wanted to make this dish for a few days now since we last met up at Starbucks for a reading a local author was hosting. Truth be told, with Kyla's busy schedule and not having anyone else to know here, Krishell had become that go-to person.

Noticing I didn't go to the store to get the jerk marinade as I had planned, I peeked into the living room to spot Kyla. Not seeing her, I walked to the back room and found her lying in bed next to Gloria. The TV was on, but neither one was watching. They both lay still, staring at different spots on the wall in silence. I let them know that I would be right back, but either one replied.

Walking out of the house, I rushed over to Krishell's door and knocked lightly. She quickly opened the door. "Hey!" she smiled and moved to the side. "What's going on with you today?" She was in her happy, cheery mood as usual. Something I have come to like about her. I started to realize at Kyla's it was usually gloomy, lonely, and routine. With Krishell, there was always something new and fresh to experience.

I was tired of the in-between where my very own emotions went up and down like a roller coaster. I had to start placing my game plan into action of get rid of Keith. Maybe that would help.

"I didn't go to the store to get that jerk marinade that you had mentioned. You got some?" I asked.

"Yeah, as a matter of fact, sure do." I followed her into her kitchen as I looked around her place. I had never stepped foot past her living room before. It was quite Afrocentric. The walls were painted green and black; African artifacts were scattered in various places. She even had beads draped across every walkway.

"Interesting decorations you have in here," I said as my head bounced from wall to wall. I admired the paintings she had up that resembled the African heritage as well.

"Just a little of my Jamaican roots," Krishell laughed. "I painted that one there myself. Got a few of mine hanging up. The ones I couldn't dare part with."

I raised an eyebrow. "You paint?"

She giggled and bowed her head bashfully as she reached in her cabinet and pulled out the ingredients I needed. "I do."

"For a minute there I was seeing African artifacts, but now remembering your Jamaican upbringing, it all makes sense. It's nice though. I like it." I sat down on a bar stool in front of her kitchen counter across from her.

"I was making some hot tea. Do you want some? I don't want to pry, my friend, but you look a little tense. Tired perhaps?"

I began to tell her about Gloria and how I didn't tell Kyla that I believed she was strung-out and whoring. I needed to find a softer way to tell her that. "I know for a fact we need to find her husband. The number Kyla had isn't working."

"I know a guy at the courthouse. I can ask him for a favor to see if they have something on this Victor, you say?"

"Yeah, Victor. I'll get some more information for you." Silence fell upon us as I began to look her over. "Oh, my bad. You're all dressed up. Am I interrupting anything?"

"Nope. Headed out in about an hour, though, if you want to get away from the drama that's in your condo. Jeez, that is some unneeded mess, and you don't even know those folks. But never mind me."

Suddenly, Krishell jumped up excitedly and grabbed my hand. "Come with me to this art showing. A poet by the name of Bashnir will be performing. The owner said he would have one of my paintings up too."

I grinned and said, "Excited, aren't we? Yeah, when is it? I could use some time to get away. Plus, I need to write on my manuscript."

She released my hand and turned to the stove to cut off the hot water she was warming for the tea and said, "Oh yeah, so has Sebastian told Linda he loves her yet?" she asked, referencing the characters in my book. I laughed and suddenly it hit me that I hadn't even had the chance to talk to Kyla about my book yet.

"No, I haven't gotten that far yet in the book. And how do you know I write the book that way anyhow?" She handed me the cup of tea as I started to blow on it to cool it down.

Laughing, she said, "Oh, I just have this feeling about it. Anyway, the event is in two hours. Are you still trying to make that pasta?"

My mouth hung halfway open for a few seconds before I said, "You know what? I could use a night out. They can eat whatever is in the fridge."

Brittany

I SAT AT my desk at work and just stared at the phone. It had become my ritual now for two days. I performed my work, went home, and did the same ritual there too. But Michael never called. Blowing out hot air I rested my head on my desk in frustration. I was just tired. Tired of waiting to see if my phone was going to ring with his name across the screen.

I eyed my phone when it suddenly rang and grabbed it like it was the last slice of that sweet potato pie Mama Lorraine makes and clicked TALK. "Hello!"

"Hey, Brit Brat."

I smiled at the sound of my sister's voice. Since leaving a few months back for the first time, after nearly a decade, we went back to our normal routine. Which is that we barely spoke, maybe a few times a month tops, and that was it. But I must admit I was glad she called me now.

"Kyla! Sis, what's up?" I was excited but immediately subconsciously took the excitement out of my voice to not seem like a kid missing her big sis.

"I'm checking on you and baby Mikey over there. It's been nothing but crazy drama here. I got to get you caught up to speed."

"Drama. Ha! You wouldn't believe the mess I got myself into."

I could hear Kyla breathing out as if she was prepping herself to hear more bad news. I didn't want to do that to her. I didn't want to add to whatever was going on with her so I asked, "Chris—how is that going now that he's in D.C.?"

"It's OK, you know. I mean, I haven't broken things off with Keith yet, so I'm like walking that fine line of a having a messed-up situation."

I laughed and said, "Sis, I think you qualify for a messed-up situation. You better stop playing with these men's hearts. Trust, I know."

"I mean, Brit, I know. It's not hard, though. I like Keith, and I love Chris."

"Wait. Did I just hear you say you like one and love the other? I'm confused."

Laughing, Kyla said, "Wait. I did say that, huh? Damn, I didn't realize this until I just spoke it."

"See, calling me was beneficial after all," I laughed. "Now, my turn."

"OK, shoot, baby girl."

I grew silent before I uttered the words. "Chance is back!"

Silence.

"Sis, did you hear me? I said Chance is back."

"Brittany, I don't know what that means, or what you want me to say. Do I need to fly back to Fort Worth to see what the hell is really going on?"

"I mean, I'm not with him or anything. He's just been helping me out here and there."

"After he fucked Tionna, or at least tried to, according to her?"

"I don't know if that's totally true." There was silence again.

"You sound like a damn fool, Brittany. You mean to tell me you don't believe your best friend over the guy you broke up with a year ago? And to top that off, you are currently pregnant by one of the greatest guys I have personally met. So what happened with Michael, because I know something happened?"

"We got into an argument. Asked me if the baby was his, and pretty much hinted that he thought it was Chance's."

I could hear Kyla blow out air before she said, "Two weeks. Give me two weeks to be out there. I will try to stay for as long as I can. Got to get some things situated with Gloria and

Chris, and I'm on my way. In the meantime, don't follow in my footsteps and leave the one who got away behind. Don't mess this up, Brittany. Talk to Michael. Do what you got to do and make it right."

"OK, Kyla, jeez, don't jump down my throat."

"Brittany, if you don't grow the hell up I *will* be jumping down more than that, and Baby Mikey will be here early." I heard the phone click without so much as a good-bye. I dropped my phone on my desk and looked at the clock. I didn't bother to wait for the ten minutes for me to be off. I grabbed my purse and phone and clocked out. I had someone to go visit.

βββ

Tapping my foot I grew impatient as I waited on her to open the door. I could hear the music blaring on the other side. Aaliyah was the song of choice. I rolled my eyes and waited patiently after knocking again.

The door swung open as I said, "Tionna, well, finally, the Queen makes her appearance." I hadn't seen her since she walked out on me at the Lyrical Lounge. Her house was dimly lit as I walked straight to the dining-room area and flicked on the nearest light. "We need to talk."

Closing the door and standing there in her skintight gym clothes I ignored my instant jealousy of her perfect figure as I battled the size of a basketball of a stomach.

"Talk!" she said. She pranced over to her couch and plopped down.

"I haven't heard from you since that stint at the lounge. You haven't called and checked on me, and I wonder why," I yelled.

Placing her glass down on the table in front of her, she leaned back on the cushion of the couch and smirked. "I was busy."

"Don't give me that, Tionna. I know when something is going on with you. Now, what's up?"

She turned her head, making a picture on the wall her focus. I followed her eyes and landed on a picture of us graduating college. My mood softened at just the sight of it. I turned my attention back to Tionna and said, "What's going on, Tionna?"

She leaned forward, placing her elbows on her knees and looked down at the floor. I sat down on the love seat across from her to ease the pain in my lower back when she finally began to speak.

"I don't know what has always been up with me. You would think that a friendship of ten years would give you automatic trust. That I would wish nothing but genuine happiness for you." She took her focus off the floor and back to me.

Tilting my head to the side I scrunched my nose as if something was funky. But the only thing that annoyed me was not a stench; it was the mysterious way Tionna was talking. It was her demeanor. It was dark, cold, and hollow. "T, what is wrong with you?" I asked.

She dropped her head and again entwined her fingers. "You seemed to always have it together, Brittany. In high school you were popular, had the guys at your feet, and then you meet

Chance. He wasn't like the dogs that came barking at me. He was actually a good one. All through high school and college he wouldn't take the bait. So I had to do what I had to do."

It was if the very life in my body began to weaken as I fell backward on the love seat and gripped my stomach. I grunted with pain and flinched. Tionna looked up and rushed over to me. "Are you OK?"

"Don't touch me!" I screamed. I placed pressure on my side to ease the discomfort I was experiencing from falling back too quickly. Scooting my rear toward the edge of the seat, I managed to stand up and stumbled backward away from Tionna.

I blew out to catch my breath as I was breathing like I had just run a mile. Fury was pouring through my temples. "Where's my purse, where's my purse?" I asked myself hysterically.

Tionna stepped back and called out, "Brit!"

I threw up my hand and ordered her to not say another word. I passed by that college graduation picture and picked it up. I looked into the eyes of those two young women full of life, excited about life after college, and supposedly the best of friends. In a matter of seconds, I threw it down to the ground, making sure the glass shattered to reflect the current state of my heart.

I turned and faced her. "You lied. That whole time you lied. You took him away from me. Damn, Tionna, the only man I loved. I haven't been able to hold a decent relationship or trust any man because I thought he betrayed me."

"I didn't take him away; you just believed what you wanted." Her voice was so robotic that I didn't even recognize it. It didn't sound like her. I shook my head in confusion. "When I saw him at the Lyrical Lounge I knew that the games were about to begin all over, and I wasn't up to playing."

"You ungrateful, sorry-ass bitch," I screamed.

She threw up her hands in surrender and rolled her eyes. "Blame me, why don't you?" She walked back over to the couch and picked up her drink again and took a swallow. "Like I said, you just believed me. If he was so great, then you wouldn't have believed one word, so who's fault is that?"

Was I hearing her right? Did I hear the dumbest but yet most truthful logic out of her mouth? But why wouldn't I believe the person who has been my rock since I was fifteen years old? I walked over behind her and grabbed a head full of hair. I pulled her head backward so that she could see me standing over her. "Move and I will pull harder," I screamed.

Her breathing was rapid as her eyes darkened with anger and fear at the same time. I took my free hand and slammed it down on her face. She jerked upward as I let go of her head. "What?" I challenged her. At this moment, I didn't care that I was almost seven months pregnant. At this moment, no baby was holding me back from whopping her ass.

"Get the hell out of here!" Tionna screamed, pointing at the door. I popped my lips, rolled my eyes a time or two, and followed her orders.

"This is not over!" I said before slamming her door behind me. That one hit wasn't good enough.

Tionna

I WALKED OVER to my front door and locked it after Brittany left. My right cheek was still burning from where she hit it. Angrily, I walked into my bathroom and grabbed a face towel and ran cold water over it. Placing the towel on my face, I stared at my reflection. Beside my hair slightly disheveled and the red burning cheek, I didn't look half bad.

I pulled the band from around my hair that was placed into a ponytail and shook my head until my hair was nearly standing all over my head. My reflection was what I was most comfortable with now. Ugly!

Then I walked out of the bathroom and made a beeline to the fridge to get a Heineken. My cell phone buzzed just as I opened it. Retrieving it, I read the text message, OPEN THE DOOR.

I threw the phone back down on the counter and walked to the front door, unlocking the locks one at a time. At first sight I sucked my teeth to show that I was annoyed by their presence.

"What the hell is up with your hair?" they asked me.

"Don't worry about that. What's up? What are you doing popping up over here anyway? I told you to stop doing that mess," I replied taking a huge gulp of my beer to help ease the tension I was currently feeling.

"Looks like I needed to call, huh? I saw little Ms. Brittany just drive off. Interesting. What is she doing over here?"

"She's starting to put two and two together, that's what." I plopped down on my couch and reached for the remote. "Did you come empty-handed, or did you at least bring some food?"

"Never mind if I brought food. Tell me what she's starting to know, Tionna. Don't tell me that you're messing up the plan. We worked months on this."

I sat straight up and screamed, "Look now, I only agreed to this damn plan because I'm tired of looking at that bitch in the face and acting like I love her and shit. Her ass will be fine without me in her life." I grabbed my beer and took another gulp.

They laughed at me and whispered, "You are one miserable, depressed, and jealous chick. Main reason why you work so well in this situation."

I rolled my eyes. "Yeah; whatever. Order me some food, will ya?" I turned my attention back to the TV and began to get lost in the program.

"I'll go pick us up some food to shoot. This baby has me eating like a fat chick these days."

I waved them off and turned the volume up on the TV to block out my thoughts on how I was betraying the only person who had genuinely loved me as they walked back out of my door. I shrugged my shoulders to myself and said out loud, "Doesn't matter. Bitches lie just like men do every day, all day." I smirked and took another gulp of my beer and went to fetch another bottle.

Keith

I WALKED INTO my bedroom to see Nadine sprawled across it. "No company tonight?" I asked. For years now we were faithful swingers, often bringing other women into our bedroom for my own sexual pleasures. After a long day at work I was looking forward to releasing some tension. But it looked as if Nadine had other plans.

"Where is everybody?" I asked, throwing my briefcase onto the chaise in our bedroom and began to loosen my tie.

"It got canceled. One couple couldn't make it, then another one canceled because they were wanted to swing with the couple that canceled. And so on, and so on." Nadine rose up from the bed and began to crawl toward me on her knees. She patted a spot on the bed and gestured for me to take a seat.

Sitting down in front of her I relaxed my shoulders as she began to massage them. I allowed my head to fall backward as I said, "Where's Gloria? I haven't seen her at the office in a couple days."

Nadine whispered, "Shhh, she'll be fine. Just got a little ruff with the last client, but she'll be OK."

I turned my head, jerking my shoulders from her reach. "Ruff? Ruff how, Nadine? Where is she?"

"She's with family she told me. I'll see her in a couple days. Don't worry, Daddy, I got this under control. Now, turn around, relax, and meet Lola."

I raised an eyebrow and just as I was about to ask who Lola was, I saw a silhouette of a woman standing to my right. I smirked at Nadine and turned around completely to see the Latina woman, petite, full in her hips, ass, and I licked my lips as my eyes made a resting place on her perky breasts.

"Lola!" I whispered. I grunted slightly to loosen the tightness in my voice, taking my hand and wrapping it around my already-hardened erection.

Lola walked over to me as a slight purring sound escaped her mouth. I could feel Nadine moving slightly away from me as I leaned backward to ease the anticipation my dick was feeling. She leaned down and kissed me fully on the lips and began humming.

"Keith, nice to meet you." With the soft whisper of her voice I nodded my head that I was happy to meet her as well. Lowering herself in front of me, she took my left hand and kissed the base of it and placed it to the left of me. She then took my right hand and repeated the same gesture and placed it to the right of me.

Scooting closer to me, she parted my legs at the knees and purred. I noticed my dick jerk at the sound of her call. She smiled, and I smirked. *This chick is going to be just what I need.*

Slowly taking her hands to search for my zipper, she pulled it down, opening the passageway to my hardened erection that was now nearly creating its only melodic rhythm before her. Her small hands reached for my hands as she gestured for me to rise up. I did as she commanded and slowly moved my pants downward as she pulled them completely off of me.

Then she lowered her head and hummed again, as if she smelled sweet scents of honey seeping from my very pores. Licking her cherry gloss-covered lips she whispered, "Relax, Keith, I'm only here to please you. Can I do that?"

I nodded my head yes without uttering a word. I could feel Nadine move away from behind me as I watched Lola lower her head. Taking my manhood into her hands, she wrapped her hands around it and gave it a firm stroke. As I watched her mouth open, my head fell back to wait for the connection of her hot mouth.

I moaned out, accepting the warm wetness of her mouth as her bobbed her head up and down. Using her right hand to stroke me with each move of her head, she pushed my hips into her mouth. Through slitted eyes I watched Nadine walk around the bed and fall down behind Lola. She pushed Lola's lace thong downward, trailing her hand down the base of her back to her ass.

Lola moaned out as Nadine snaked her finger inside of her. Watching Nadine please Lola sent my ecstasy in overdrive as I began to jab myself aggressively inside of Lola's mouth, moving down her throat. I filled her mouth and throat. I couldn't hold back as I witnessed Lola had no gag reflex. My seeds rapidly exploded in her mouth.

The perfect way to begin my evening before my night out with Kyla.

Kyla

I PULLED MY hair behind my ear and allowed my head to fall backward. The night breeze blew over my chilled cheeks as I released tension with each breathe I blew out. The weight of my shoulders was causing agony, not only physically but mentally. I was beyond the point of being tired. I was utterly exhausted.

"You look tired, babe." Keith sat next to me on the bench in the park that we had decided to come to.

"I am," I dryly responded. It had been days since I had found Gloria in a house with a strange man who nearly ran me over as he plowed past me. It had been days with no answers and no way of finding Gloria's husband Victor. I was stuck. I was confused. I was blindsided.

"What's on your mind?" Keith brought his hands to my shoulders and began to massage them. I pressed my back forward, letting him know I was accepting his touch.

"Gloria!"

He was speechless for a moment, and then he asked, "Where has she been? I haven't seen her at the office."

"I took Gloria to her sister's house the day before last and have been checking in on her, but she won't come to the phone." I paused and blew out air trying to fight my own tears. "I think she has gotten into something."

"Something like what?"

I dropped my head and made the pavement my new focus. "Let's just run another mile. I really don't want to talk about it. Plus, Chris and I . . ." I trailed off my words forgetting who it was I was talking to.

"Chris!" Keith raised an eyebrow and jerked up as if suddenly he felt ants attacking his ass.

"Um, yeah, we're going out. Just food," I stated. Keith raised a curious eyebrow and ran his palms across his thighs. I added, "So one more run around the track?"

"This kind of explains his behavior toward me at the game the other day."

"Behavior? He didn't tell me anything."

He chuckled arrogantly and said, "I must be a fool to not see that y'all two are fucking. Damn, makes me look like a damn fool."

"You got all of that from me saying we were getting something to eat?" I asked, halfway annoyed, trying to defend my case.

Keith walked a few steps away from me before turning around and saying, "What did you tell him to make him agree to this damn arrangement you obviously had. Him, then me? Damn, you women are a trip." With my mouth half open from shock I watched Keith get in his car and pull off.

Him getting upset was just too easy; I got to figure out what was said at that game they went to.

βββ

I pulled up in front of my condominium and turned the engine off. It was an early night, and it was supposed to have been spent with Keith, while Chris was off to the coffee shop to write. Maybe Keith walking away was the push I needed to make a decision. I picked up my cell phone to look at the time and saw that it was early enough to call and check on Brittany. When she didn't answer, I sent her a text.

Trying to block Brittany's current situation out of my head, I pushed myself back into the driver's seat and exhaled loudly once again. I didn't want to go inside and start a confrontation, but something had to be said. This man came from clear across the country waiting on me to make a decision. I had once loved his brother, then him, now Keith. Wait—did I love Keith? I don't even know if I got there yet. I know he made me feel special; he took my mind off of all of my worries. He was my escape. But maybe I never fell in love because I still had love there for Chris.

I picked up my cell and dialed Chris's number. Three rings, and then voice mail. I threw it down on the passenger seat and allowed the silence of the night to take over me once again. And just when I thought my night couldn't get any worse . . . out walked Chris. He wasn't alone.

Chris

TAKING THE BAG out of Krishell's hand I gripped it in mine and waited for her to lock her front door. I had to admit I was excited about tonight. Krishell had been invited to attend an art showing with live music and offered to bring me along. I was going to write a similar scene in my book and figured this would also add great research that I would need.

"Don't drop my bag now; it has valuable things in it," Krishell joked.

I glanced at it and shook my head. "Looks like a lot of sketches you have yet to finish." She extended her hand and asked for the bag back, which I refused. "I'll carry this, lady, to your car. Now, where are you parked?"

She pointed to a red Camry, and I led the way. Opening her door first, I hurriedly walked around and got into the passenger seat.

"You seem all giddy, like a big kid," she joked.

"Finally happy to get out of the house today. Bored and I didn't have much luck looking for work either."

Pulling out of the parking area she said, "Well, I know of this guy who could use some help at an ad agency. I think it's a temp position, but it's something."

I nodded my head that I would love the opportunity as she turned on the latest R&B jam. After fighting D.C. traffic for forty-five minutes, we pulled into the parking lot of the gallery and hopped out.

Dressed in black slacks, a silver shirt, and black blazer, I was freshly cut and shaven as well and wearing just the right amount of Calvin Klein. I was feeling myself. I began to run my hands over my pants, removing invisible wrinkles and cracked my knuckles in nervousness. Krishell grabbed my hand and said, "Boy, please, you actually look pretty hot. I may have to force myself to look away." With a wink and a hearty laugh, she led me into the showroom, our fingers entwined with each other.

My eyes searched the room as I admired the art that was displayed. Some reflected an acoustic soul, others African heritage, while some, I just couldn't figure out. I stood in front of one for what seemed like an eternity as Krishell went off to talk to one of her friends.

"Looks weird, huh?"

I turned my head to the left of me and was approached by a woman not too much older than I. Maybe early thirties. The tall statue I was standing in front of was slightly intimidating as I nodded my head that I agreed with her. "It could be a woman cradling her baby, or a man cutting down a tree," I joked.

"That has no resemblance at all," she laughed.

"Hey, I'm not usually the one to come to these things; it's cool. The wine is good though," I added.

"Oh yeah, so who was the genius that dragged you here?"

I turned and pointed toward Krishell. "That's my friend over there."

She nodded her head and smiled, "Oh, Krishell is a triple threat. Artist, writer, and overall the perfect example of a woman who defines Afrocentric. How did you two become friends?"

"She lives next to my, well . . . one of my friends. We share that common ground of writing," I added.

"You write too?" She raised a curious eyebrow and smiled.

"Yeah, novels though, not poetry. Working on a manuscript now. That's why I came tonight too. I wanted to research and experience a scene like this."

Looking over my shoulder she said, "Oh, here comes Krishell now."

I turned around and made room for Krishell to stand between us and said, "This is . . . Wait, I'm sorry. I didn't get your name." I turned to the woman I had held a conversation with for the past ten minutes.

She extended her hand and said, "How rude of me. Krishell already knows me. But my name is Nadine."

I nodded my head. "Nadine. Cool, cool. It's really nice to meet you."

Krishell

I GAVE HER the evil eye and had hoped she would walk away. But she was always stern like that. Keeping her place in line and never backing down. I looked at Chris who was clearly clueless and told him I would return in a sec and signaled for Nadine to follow me.

Nadine walked behind me and placed her hands on both sides of my shoulders and whispered, "Beautiful art showing. Are you performing tonight too? I mean, the poetry, that is." She smirked as I tried to hide the look of disgust on my face.

"Take your hands off of me, Nadine, and, yes, I will be performing something a little later, but before I do, why you don't go ahead and make your little exit up and out of here. I don't need you or this vibe." I took my finger and pointed from her head to her feet.

Nadine had to have been around 5'11, fairly thick in all the right places. She always wore low-cut shirts that expose the 40 DD natural breasts that she wore with pride. Her long weave was jet-black with loose curls down her shoulders. The honey-colored gloss on her lips completed her chocolate tone. She was beautiful, that was true, but she was also my former boss in a field I had continuously tried to leave behind.

"Now is this the way you treat your sister?" she smirked as her full lips spread thin across her face. Her cheeks began to rise up, as if she were being bashful. I rolled my eyes.

Changing the subject quickly I asked, "Keith isn't with you?"

"No, apparently he had a late business meeting, or perhaps with the bitch Kyla."

I rolled my eyes. "I have no clue why you are jealous of any other woman he sleeps with anyway. He's never leaving you. This we both know." I grabbed a wineglass from a server walking by and handed it to her. "Take a sip, relax, and then leave," I hinted again, letting her know that I wanted her gone.

She took a large gulp of the wine and winced at its strong contents and took a deep breath. "I'm waiting on you to move faster on this. I promised to let you go once you did what I asked."

"Look, Nadine, I appreciate you and all that for taking me when I first got out of high school. Giving me shelter, food, and, I guess, you can call it a job. But don't rush me on this. Chris is a good guy, and I don't think he knows what he's up against. I will get it done, just don't be popping up around here." I took the glass out of her hand and gulped the last of its contents.

"Well, I guess I'll leave. But I won't be far away."

Rolling my eyes and giving her the fakest smile, I said, "This I know, Nadine. Now get!"

Brittany

I KNOCKED LIGHTLY and waited. Mama Lorraine opened the door just when I felt my bladder couldn't hold any longer. "Hey, Mama, give me a minute." I rushed past her and made my way to the closest bathroom. After relieving myself I wandered back into the living area only to find Mama in the kitchen.

Sitting down at the kitchen table I asked, "What are you cooking?"

She placed an onion on her cutting board and said, "Joe is coming over. Going to make him a Southern-style dinner. Everything fattening and saturated with salt." She laughed, and then looked over toward me, "You look tired. Are you getting enough rest?"

"I get enough," I mumbled. "So date night for you and Mr. Joe? I won't stay long then."

"Girl, hush. You can stay as long as you want. I changed the sheets on your old bed a couple days ago if you feel like resting there. Clean towels in the closet, everything you need," she said placing the onions in a frying skillet.

Laughing, I exhaled and said, "OK, Mama, I surely will do that." Walking up the stairs I heard her add she would call me once the food was ready. It was just what I needed, for my Mama to baby her baby who was carrying her baby.

I opened the door to the room I had lived in from when I was a kid until I went to college. I turned my head to look toward where Kyla's room was, and it tugged at my heart to always see it empty. Mama used it as a storage room now. Walking in, I laughed to myself at the decorations that still covered the walls. The mind of a sixteen-year-old had old pictures of the group B2K all over the walls.

Kicking off my shoes, I plopped down on the bed and sat in silence. This night was hell. It's one thing to have a man break your heart, but to have your best friend hurt you, how do you heal from that?

Picking up my cell I saw a text from Kyla. I replied back telling her I was at Mama's house. She texted back in less than five minutes and said she would be Texas-bound sooner than I thought. Raising an eyebrow, I became curious to know what was going on in her world but decided to ask about that another time. I was in need of a hot bath.

βββ

I jerked at the sound of a dish hitting the floor. Groaning, I stretched over to the other side of my bed and reached for my phone. It was two A.M. After bathing and eating, I had marched right on up to my room and left Mama and Mr. Joe alone. Apparently, they were still up.

I rubbed away the sleep in my eyes and called out to Mama to make sure everything was OK. She instantly put on her boss hat and demanded that I go back to sleep as I heard laughter from her and Mr. Joe echo throughout the house.

Noticing a light blinking on my phone I picked it up and went straight to my messages. *Chance!*

He sent me a message an hour ago that only said, HEY, HIT ME BACK. Wonder what he wanted. I replied with one word: SLEEP.

Lying back down and closing my eyes it was only mere seconds before the ringing of my phone began. My mood went from sleepy and full of Mama's cooking to annoyed. "Yeah!"

"I haven't heard from you all day, are you OK?" Chance asked.

"I just messaged you and told you I was asleep and now you call. What's up, Chance? I'm good, now a little annoyed, but was totally fine."

"I mean, I'm guessing you had a rough day and needed someone to talk to. I found it odd that I didn't hear from you."

Pausing, I sucked my teeth and didn't let up on my attitude. "Rough day? Why would you have that impression?"

"I'm just saying you would text or something. You and ole dude doing OK?"

"Chance, really, it's almost three in the morning. I'm tired. Bug me about my new relationship tomorrow," I said sarcastically and hung up. I know he didn't do anything wrong, but right now, I didn't want to be bothered with anyone. Not even the man who I dumped based off of a lie.

Michael

I WAVED AT the bartender and said to give me another. I wasn't in the mood to have small talk with anyone. I didn't want to be bothered with the random women that found their way by me to ask me for my name. I wasn't answering any clients' calls either. I was busy. Busy in my own thoughts and in my own world.

"That's your fourth one." I knew the alcohol was taking over my mind now. I was hallucinating. Her voice was ringing in my ears like I had just heard her speak yesterday. Turning in my seat I jerked just a little as my sudden moves reminded me that I had drunk just a little too much alcohol.

She turned to the bartender and said, "Jimmie, I got him. Bring me a bottle of water."

Jimmie the bartender replied, "Yes, Boss, I was going to call you up here. I know you two used to be cool back in the day."

I mumbled, "I should have known I would run into you here, this being your lounge and all. But I thought you moved to Houston."

Placing her hand on my shoulder, Nitrah replied, "I did move, there, to check on the place and family. And apparently you too." She laughed slightly and handed me my bottle of water.

I hadn't seen her in years. Nitrah! Just the sound of her name still makes me hard in my dick as well as my heart. I had loved her once. Wanted to be with her forever and that didn't pan out to be the truth after going back and forth with my former best friend Troy. When she couldn't choose between us, I walked away, moving to Toronto and several places after that.

"I'm good, Nitrah, don't need a babysitter."

She threw up her hands in surrender and turned to Jimmie and ordered some buffalo wings. "I want you to put something on your stomach. This will make me feel better."

"Hey, it's free, so I ain't tripping," I laughed. I suddenly felt the beginning of a headache and winced. Nitrah started to fumble through her purse and pulled out some Tylenol. She handed it to me, and I couldn't hold back my laughter. "Still taking care of me."

"Hey, that's what former girlfriends are for." She watched me take the pills, and we sat in silence for a couple of minutes when she continued, "So what happened?"

"One word—women."

Nitrah laughed out again. "Hey, tell me about it. I have had to let some of you knuckleheads go as well as my so-called best friends. Women, huh? What's her name?"

I went on to tell her about Brittany and LeAnn and how everything seemed to be going wrong. And I appreciated that all Nitrah did was listen. She didn't interrupt me or tell me what she thought I should do. She just nodded her head and listened. It felt good to get most of this mess off of my chest.

"I don't think that baby is mine."

"I wouldn't go that far. You never gave ole girl a chance to explain. See, even I had to learn to stop walking away and let the other person talk. Even your dumb-ass former friend Troy," she laughed.

"How is Nina?" Thinking of Troy and I reminded me that they had a child together. A child I once wished was mine.

"She is so big and beautiful. Here, take this pic of her." She opened up her wallet and pulled out a picture of Nina. It had been years; she was so grown now and looked just like her mother. Even though Troy was as yellow as they came, Nitrah was the darkest woman I had ever dated. Smooth chocolate skin with the brightest smile. Nina had her mama's skin color.

I put the picture in my pocket and thanked her. We began to snack on the wings she had ordered and caught up with each other and what we had been up to over the years.

"Let me call your boys Tim and Robert. Hey, maybe even Troy will show up." Nitrah pulled out her phone.

I chuckled slightly at the idea of Troy's best friend Tim and brother Robert coming to meet up with me after all of this time. Instead, I told Nitrah that's OK. We exchanged numbers after she called me a cab and told me to call her if I needed anything while she was still in town. Kissing her on the cheek I thanked her for listening and told her I would keep her posted on my situation.

Tipping the bartender I walked outside to my cab and went straight to Omar's house. I needed a night out, and the night was young.

βββ

After changing, Omar and I were now standing at the bar of Club Reign. The music was playing the latest hit from rapper J Smooth, and I laughed and tapped Omar on the shoulder. "Yo, man, this is my night for a trip down memory lane."

I pointed toward the DJ booth and saw Denim, or as the public calls him now, DJ Denim O. Originally from Fort Worth as well, I remembered now that he produced J Smooth and oftentimes DJ'd his appearances. I pointed toward him, directing Omar to look toward that direction. When noticing him he laughed, and then asked me if I wanted to leave. "Dude, I just saw Nitrah earlier. So I guess they are both in town to see each other or something."

Denim was Nitrah's ex and one of the main reasons why being with her made me insecure. They always double-dipped back with each other. I told Michael that I was cool with staying but made sure Denim didn't see me in the crowd.

"Wanna dance?" I heard a small voice from behind me and turned to see who it was.

I exaggeratedly blew out air and jerked backward from her reach. Omar saw her and said, "Damn, bitch, you ain't got somewhere to be?"

Raising my hand and pushing him backward by his chest I interjected, "Yo, bro, don't do that. She's pregnant, man."

"Yeah, I'm pregnant with your nephew, Omar," LeAnn added.

Omar threw up his hands and shouted over the music to the bartender to get him another beer. "Get rid of this psycho, bro, before I go off."

Wanting to defuse the situation I asked, "What's up, LeAnn? We meet next week to get a fetal DNA test, so I am not even going to assume we just randomly 'happened' to be at the same club. Speaking of clubs, you are way too pregnant to be in here."

"Yeah, don't know other niggas in here want you," Omar added.

"Hey, I can dance and shake my booty." She laughed and shook her hips from left to right.

Totally disgusted and thrown off by her behavior I replied, "Just walk away and go on with whatever you were doing. I'll see you next week."

"OK, Daddy. I will this one time." She waved a childish good-bye as if she were an adolescent and wobbled away.

"That woman is crazy, bro. You got to handle that," Omar said handing me another beer.

"Oh, it's handled. Come next week, this woman is out of my life." I opened the bottle of beer and just as I had it midway to my mouth I noticed LeAnn walk over to a familiar face.

Omar noticed who I was looking at and said, "Tionna. Now what the fuck does she and LeAnn have in common?"

Anger began to take over my entire being as I noticed them embrace like they were the best of friends. "I don't know, bro, but this mess is starting to get crazier by the minute." I took out my cell phone and zoomed in on them too. In one click I had evidence of my enemy with my girl's best friend.

Now I wasn't drinking from pure anger as I was earlier. I was downing my beer with pure confusion. This just wasn't making any sense.

Kyla

CALL ME CRAZY. *OK, don't call me crazy because I know a fishy situation when I see one. My next-door neighbor knows Nadine. Putting two and two together, my guess is that it's not a coincidence.* I was trying to play back the scenario in my head. Nadine was extrafriendly in my Zumba class. But she only came a few times before she stopped. And now I wondered how my neighbor, who was obviously trying to woo Chris, knew Nadine, but I couldn't find a connection.

Then my vision zoomed in on Chris. Was he in on whatever these chicks were cooking up? I pushed downward in my seat to watch the view. I hadn't planned on following Chris, but I was glad I did.

I heard the buzzing of my phone and noticed a text from Brittany. I let her know I was coming sooner than I expected. I then began to search through my contacts and Gloria's name came up. I missed her. I was lost without her, and I still didn't know what happened.

She wouldn't say any more than two words to me and only wanted to go to her sister's house. So I took her, and since then, I haven't heard from her. I texted her phone with the simple word of a hello and hoped for the best.

Taking my attention back to the art gallery, my eyes began to wander frantically. Now I didn't see anyone. My heart began to flutter in the pit of my belly as I began to believe that I had taken my attention away from them too long. That was, until I spotted Chris and the neighbor again, but no Nadine.

"Shoot!" I threw my hand onto the dashboard. Then I plopped back in my seat and watched Chris and my neighbor exchange friendly chatter. Watching them was boring. I hate to admit it, but I was waiting to get confirmation of Chris dogging me out with her. I yearned to see him touch her gently, her flirt obvious, bringing attention to her breasts, a simple kiss on the lips, or a sense of flirtation. But these two were so platonic I grew annoyed.

I did say don't call me crazy, huh? I developed a childish attitude and folded my arms across my chest as I continued to look on. Minutes turned to hours, and now I was hungry. I began to laugh at myself out loud from the mere thought of hoping to catch Chris cheating, and I knew why. I wanted an easy way out. A way to tell him to return to Fort Worth and out of my life.

Maybe I could give Keith what he wanted. A commitment. But that relationship was on the verge of ending. How did I start out not having a date or a decent lay in months before getting with

Keith to juggling a relationship with him and the brother of my first love?

My mind then began to wander to Dean, Chris's brother and my first love. Our relationship was nonexistent now. I was now living clear across the country with his brother. And oddly, for that moment, I had missed him. I began to shake my head in shame. How could I miss the man who turned out to be married and his wife tried to shoot me dead?

Life was a joke, and the crazy thing is that I wasn't laughing. None of this shit was funny. I swear I wanted to take a hammer and bash someone across the skull. Just watch it create a big-ass dent in their head to take away the massive weight that was on my head. I began to clutch at my chest and sigh.

I was tired of this merry-go-round. I was away from my sis who going through so much and with only a mere 2½ months before the baby was here I wanted to be there for her.

I picked up my phone and called my bother Sean who also lived in D.C. "Sean, are you going to take that trip with me?"

Sean laughed and said, "Baby sis, you still trying to get me to go back to Texas?"

"Let's go see Mama and Brittany. Stop being stubborn. Pack up your wife and kids and let's go."

He paused and took in the hint of sadness in my voice and asked, "Sis, you OK?"

"You wouldn't believe the mess I'm going through." I pulled out of the parking lot and began to tell him the story of how suddenly Nadine was a person of interest and more than likely holds the answers to all of my questions. But finding her, now *that* was my next agenda.

Brittany

MAMA HAD MADE me comfortable lying in my old bed, in my old house, and I was being a big baby, only getting up to use the bathroom and eat. I had decided to take off work for a week just to luxuriate. I sat in Mama's big house all alone while she was off working the night shift and found myself wondering why she continues to live here all those years after Daddy died and after Kyla and Sean moved away.

I took the remote in my hand and began to flip through the channels when I heard the doorbell ring. The lazy bone in my head debated on if I should get up and answer it or not. I decided to get up. After three tries of failing to rise, I rolled to my right side and pushed upward. This baby was wearing thin on my body, and I was tired of it.

"Yeah, who is it?" I yelled.

"Hey, Brit Brat, open up."

I sucked my teeth and blew out exaggerated air from my lungs. Swinging the door open I yelled, "Fool, really?" I had no idea why he was here at the doorstep of my mother's house.

"Brit, move to the side. I brought you some Papi's."

I raised an eyebrow, "Papi's? From my favorite Cuban cuisine spot?" I looked at the door and back at him as he walked through and headed for the living room. "Don't act like you own the place," I yelled behind him, closing the door.

"I'm not, woman. I just remember Mama Lorraine always inviting me in to watch *Sparkle* with her." He laughed at the mention of my mother's favorite movie she watched constantly.

"Anyway, what did you get me? My favorite steak?"

"Steak? That's too much for the baby. Got you some chicken instead. Go ahead and sit down. I'll go grab us some plates."

I rolled my eyes and protested the chicken even though I knew I was going to eat it. Taking in my first huge bite, Chance popped in the movie, *Love & Basketball,* and it was like the old days all over again.

"Now how long are you planning on staying? You know I fall asleep early these days," I asked.

"Well, since Mama's gone, I can stay with you through the night, and then leave once she's about to come home. Cool?"

I bet he had this planned from when we talked earlier, and I told him Mama was gone for the night. The hell if I cared. I ended up getting some free food.

I contemplated his proposition a little bit before agreeing. Then I pulled a blanket up to my chin and lay my head on the biggest pillow I could find and rested my feet in Chance's lap. In a matter of minutes, he was massaging my swollen feet. And I was out like faded sunshine.

Chance

I COULDN'T SIT here and tell you that I didn't have an agenda. It didn't matter that the woman I had loved all those years was carrying another man's child. The child could become my son; I could be his dad. If I was willing to bite my tongue and wait for Brittany to come back to me, then I could have that chance. But waiting wasn't an option.

I sat there watching her as the TV played in the background. She was still comfortable around me, she still allowed me here with her, and she still allowed me to take care of her. She wasn't admitting it out of her mouth just yet, but she still had love for me. You can't let go of our history like that in a year.

Wrapping my hands around her feet, I warmed her cold soles with the palms of my hands. All I kept thinking of was that I had helped Michael have her. If I hadn't walked away so easily, then this wouldn't be the issue at hand. She wouldn't be carrying his child. It would be ours.

I attempted to block out the fact that this was what I was left with now, a huge challenge. I began to massage her toes one toe at a time, creating a deep movement into the core muscles of her feet. I wanted her to relax more than I had ever wanted. I heard slight moans escape her mouth as the rhythm of my hands trailed from her soles to her calves. I deepened my rhythm increasing my efforts to make her feel as if her body weren't her own.

I had whispered her name to see just how awake she was. She didn't reply to my calling her name. She just lay there stretched from one end of the couch to the other, including my lap. I grunted slightly as the pressure began to weigh in on me. The anxiety from touching just the base of her body was beginning to get to me. She was pregnant, this was true, but it was still her. She still had this golden glow on her skin that mimics the trails of honey.

I still had that same desire to want to touch her in a way that I knew would send her to an orgasmic release. I wanted so badly to remember how it was when our bodies connected as one. When my heartbeat was identical to her heartbeat. My breathing became erratic as my intense massage in her calves traveled to her thighs. I began to breathe heavily out of my mouth to ease the anxiety. It slightly helped.

I whispered her name again to see if I could get a reply. I needed to see how alert she was. I wanted to know if she knew that the mere fact that I was touching her skin was causing me to harden. I glanced down and saw the affects bulging through my pants. The bulge was the confirmation I needed to see that I was in full salute. I needed to penetrate her; I wanted to connect with her. But how could I? I waited to see if she would answer the calling of her name.

My hands were frozen on her thighs; the room fell to a dead silence. Suddenly, I couldn't hear the sounds of the TV in the background; I didn't hear my own breathing escaping my very own mouth. I didn't hear anything as I waited for that reply.

Minutes felt like hours as I noticed movement under her covers. I jerked my head to look in her direction and stared at her silhouette. It was as if this was the very moment I knew I would get the answer I had been waiting for. Poking her head out over her right shoulder she looked at me. She didn't say a word. She didn't even blink. She just lay there and stared. I returned the stare and didn't speak either. Words didn't have to be spoken for us to know what we were thinking.

In one breath I said, "Turn on your back."

In a few shuffles and a scoot she lay on her back, her belly hiding any visual of her face. I took my eyes from her pregnant stomach to where my hands were planted and began to massage her there once again. With each movement I neared her nectar for which I hungered. I wanted to touch her there so badly that the pulsating in my hardness became unbearable. I unzipped my pants and pulled myself out to create a sense of relief.

Inch by inch, I brought my hands closer to where I needed to be. Finally, the tips of my fingers connected with her lace panties. I didn't hesitate to begin to pull them down and once at her ankles, I completely pulled them off and tossed them by her feet. I took my attention back to her and took a deep breath in. I could smell her begin to dance in the air.

The sweet smell of her sent me in a short spasm. I began to tease her clit with the tip of my head. She was so wet that the warm liquids caused me to nearly climax. Dipping my head low I began to descend closer and closer. The smell of her nectar was strong, and with a lick of my lips, I slightly parted her legs and leaned in.

I kissed her wetted lips slowly and carefully to savor this very moment. I could feel the shaking of her legs as I opened my mouth wider to allow my tongue to invade her lips. Moving in slowly and meticulously, I wrote my name between her lips, pulling her clit between my teeth and biting down on it softly.

When I felt the shakiness of her legs, I became more aggressive, ignoring the obvious river flowing out of her and onto the sofa cushions as I hungrily feasted on her. Her warm cream suddenly became the only nourishment I needed to survive this life. It was giving me life, energy, and a purpose. I grabbed her thighs and pulled her down closer to me, pushing my nose and mouth into her.

I was hungry, I was horny, and I was finally where I needed to be.

Michael

DROPPING MY HANDS into my lap, I read a text from Brittany. I had missed our doctor's appointment. She was eight months now. I hadn't seen her since I walked out on her with another man there. I shook my head to hopefully get rid of the doubt I had in my heart. *It is my baby*, I kept telling myself. But the more I said it, the less I believed it.

I didn't have time to think about how big my supposedly child probably was now. I didn't want to guess his weight, his inches, if his head was as big as mine. I didn't want to make sure he has ten fingers and ten toes. I was done for now. I had to be so that I could live. Tired of the bullshit.

I looked at the e-mail on my desk computer from my realtor titled, *Papers to close on your new home*. I sent her a simple reply that said I was pulling my offer and no longer wanted to buy. Then I deleted the message and turned my computer off. It was almost noon.

I grabbed my briefcase and walked out to my receptionist. "I'm gone for the day, and I'll call if I'm returning, but place all of my messages on my desk."

I headed toward the elevator after waving good-bye to a few colleagues on my floor and walked to the parking garage to head off to judgment day. I knew why I had forgotten about Brittany's doctor's appointment. I had taken LeAnn to go get the fetal paternity test. Today I was getting the results.

Taking her to the best doctor in Dallas, I was confident that my results wouldn't be mishandled. With each heavy step I took closer to my vehicle I was certain that this nightmare was coming to an end.

βββ

I had set down the bottle of water that was handed to me by the receptionist. With one leg crossed over my knee, I ignored LeAnn's stares. Clearing my throat, I took out my cell phone and decided to return Brittany's text after all. I didn't want to say where I was or why I didn't show up, so I simply sent the word: SORRY!

"Mr. Williams, the doctor will see you now," the receptionist called out to me. I looked up and nodded my head toward her. My attention then was directed to LeAnn who had the most hideous smirk on her face. I scrunched my face in confusion mixed in with disgust. *I cannot wait until I don't have to see this face any more.*

I stood up and extended my hand signaling for LeAnn to lead the way into the office.

"Here we go!" she announced as if she were a kid getting ready to set foot in Disney World.

I shook my head in embarrassment as the receptionist noticed LeAnn's odd behavior and shook her head as well. I walked a few feet behind LeAnn to distance myself. I hate to admit it, but I visualized my yanking her by the back of her head and slamming her up against the wall. I was ashamed of the thought, this I know.

"Mr. Williams, Ms. Dempsey, welcome. Please have a seat."

I followed the doctor's orders and took a seat across from LeAnn, who leaned back in her seat and began to rub her belly.

The doctor looked at LeAnn and down toward her stomach. "Growing and getting big, aren't we?" He gave her an innocent smile.

"Oh yes, she is growing and just about ready to pop."

I shook my head at LeAnn for announcing for the first time that the baby was a girl and also insinuating that she was almost due. Her time stamp just didn't match up to when we slept together, and I was now ready to end this nightmare.

"Doc, the answer!" I interrupted.

The doctor turned his attention back to me and smiled. "But of course, sir, and I know why you are so eager. I have taken the liberty of printing out two copies of the results and also the estimated time of arrival for this bundle of joy. Ms. Dempsey, would you like to do the honors?"

He extended his hand and handed her a folded piece of white paper. My eyes were set on it as if I was certain that someone was going to try to make it disappear at this very moment and ruin my chances of knowing the truth.

LeAnn smiled genuinely and opened and looked look at the paper so quickly I didn't have time to react to her holding the answer. She raised an eyebrow and smirked. My heart dropped. I was prepping myself to have the world end at this very moment.

"Well, that's a doozy," she called out. Her voice was like a little girl without a care in the world. Her joking demeanor disgusted me so much that I angrily reached over and snatched the paper out of her hand.

I zoomed in on the words. 99.9% NOT A MATCH. I tilted my head to the side and looked up at LeAnn, and then the doctor. "The kid isn't mine. I knew it." I threw the paper in LeAnn's face as if I was throwing dollars in the club.

The doctor pushed himself back from his desk as if he was preparing for me to do something crazy. But I threw up my hands in surrender. "I'm cool, Doc." I turned my head and looked at LeAnn who still had the same smirk on her face.

I jerked backward in confusion. This woman was crazy, and it was clearly showing in all her reactions to the results. It was as if she wasn't fazed by the results, as if she didn't care.

LeAnn stood up and smiled. "Well, my work is done here. It was nice knowing you, Michael." She threw up two fingers and said, "Deuces!"

I called out as my head jumped back from the doctor to her as she walked out of his office. "What the hell?"

The doctor added, "Well, now, that just didn't end the way I thought it would."

I looked at the doctor and said, "Doc, you best believe there is more to that. I am no fool. Something else is wrong with this picture. It's like she already knew the outcome. And if she did, why did she take it this far?"

I stood there puzzled until I could manage to move my feet and walk out of the building. One word came to mind as I hopped in my car. Tionna!

Chris

I SAT AT the coffee house with my laptop open. I was destined to write five thousand words today on my manuscript. The coffee I was digesting was fueling me for the long haul. I was amped and ready to finally write the scene I had witnessed at the art gallery. Just as I was prepping to power up my laptop my phone buzzed.

"Where are you?" Kyla asked without so much of a hello.

"At Starbucks working. What's wrong?"

"The one on 15th Street NW? I'm coming to scoop you up. Be outside in five minutes."

The phone clicked off before I could manage to say another word. I gathered my things and went to go wait outside. In a matter of minutes, Kyla pulled up. I opened the passenger-side door and got in.

"Kyla, are you OK?" She seemed eager to pull off as if she was in a rush. I didn't understand the urgent call or the urgent driving she was now doing.

"Krishell!" she said. I jumped at the sound of her mentioning that name. I looked at the side of her face to read her expression. *Does she think I'm sleeping with Krishell?* OK, so it had crossed my mind before, but I hadn't even attempted to do anything. What man wouldn't think about sex with a woman? That's just what we do. But I loved Kyla; I wasn't going to do anything to jeopardize us being together.

"You know about my hanging out with Krishell!" I said it as a statement because I wasn't about to play dumb, and I knew good and well if she was mentioning that name, then she knew I was with her on some nights. But to be honest, she was my company. She showed me her world, a world that was a lot similar to mine. I enjoyed her company. With knowing only Kyla here in D.C., she was my outlet to other companionships.

"I don't want to go into what you two have been or not doing. I just want to take you some place. I need you to see something that hopefully you can help me make sense of."

I grew nervous as I heard Kyla talk. She just seemed too calm and too mysterious. "I never slept with her or touched her in a sexual way, Kyla. We just hung out. She was company, that's all." I know that wouldn't make her feel any better.

I turned my head to see if my luggage was in the backseat. *Is she dropping me off at the airport and forcing me to go back to Texas?* "Kyla, say something!"

"I'm not mad. I'm curious. Once you see what I mean, you will wonder to. I have followed Krishell because I saw you that night with her at the art gallery. And then, I saw another woman approach you."

I began to think back to that night. Then it clicked. "Oh yeah, her friend, Na . . . something like that."

"Nadine!"

I replied as if I had just heard the winning answer to the lottery. "Yeah, that's it!" Then I grew confused. "Wait, how did you know that?"

"I met Nadine a few months back. Listen to this and tell me if this shit is crazy, OK?"

I nodded my head slowly and said, "OK!"

"I first met Nadine months back in a Zumba class. She was extrafriendly, mad cool, I thought, but then one day, she stopped coming. Then I see her out of the blue at Woodlake Park when Gloria and I were running. Now that I think about it, Gloria was shaken up by the sight of her and just disappeared and left me at the park. I had to hunt her down at her house to find her, then I find she's with a man she still has never told me about. Her husband Victor is MIA, and now Gloria has quit her job and isn't returning my phone calls."

"OK, this does sound a little crazy, but why did you mention Krishell?"

"The night at the art gallery Nadine shows up, and it was obvious Krishell knew her. So this shit is making me go crazy. I started to follow my little ole neighbor Krishell and found an apartment she and Nadine meet up at every Wednesday at three."

I looked at the clock. It was 2:45. "We're on our way there, aren't we?" It clicked that's where we were going.

"If Nadine was in my class befriending me, turns up and spooks Gloria, and then suddenly is friends with my neighbor, something ain't right. This shit ain't making sense, and I am the common denominator."

I sat back in my seat and thought about what Kyla just said. "This doesn't make sense." I started to think on how I met Krishell and wondered if that had something to do with this Nadine chick as well. I started to shake those thoughts out of my head, however. I did not want to believe that I was a part of some plan. That Krishell wasn't this person I thought I knew, and that she was out for a motive of some sorts. I wanted to believe that she was just a friend who was showing me something new in life. "What are you planning on doing?"

"Sit back and watch to see if some dots connect. I brought you with me for backup. You needed to see that Krishell obviously had an agenda, and we both need to find out why."

Brittany

I LEFT MAMA'S house even before she could return. I had Chance leave only a matter of minutes after . . . after the encounter. I stood in my own shower now in my own apartment in my own silence. Trapped in my very own thoughts. I couldn't imagine what had happened last night. I allowed old emotions and feelings to get the best of me, and I allowed Chance to . . .

My thoughts trailed off. As the blazing water splashed on my skin, I continued my daze. It seemed that with every blink of an eye that I took I was reliving the previous night's acts.

Blink. Eyes on my thighs.

Blink. His hands gripping my hips.

Blink. His mouth planted in the center of my pussy.

Blink blink blink. My memory was playing back over and over like a bad movie. I screamed out in frustration.

Taking my hand, I turned the already-blazing water to a raging inferno. I wanted to sting to deflect my thoughts. I began to rub my hands over my belly and embrace my son. I wanted to say I'm sorry for last night. I didn't want to think of him being pushed or jabbed on the inside while I allowed lust and desire to take over my entire being.

I was lonely. I was sad. I was vulnerable. My embarrassment for last night began to turn into anger toward Chance. He knew I was vulnerable, so why would he do it? Why would he even come to Mama's house where he knew I would be to escape the loneliness of my own walls in my apartment?

I reached for the soap and began to lather it up to place the suds onto my skin. Washing away any evidence of last night. I needed so much for this to just be a dream. Not a dream—a damn nightmare. *What the hell did I do?*

I called out to myself, "Brittany, get it together. You cannot let last night take control of you."

After rinsing, I cut the shower off and grabbed a big towel off of the towel rack, wrapping my body. Then I stood in front of the mirror and wiped the steam away. My reflection of disheveled hair and deep circles around my eyes was the image I now saw.

I began to rub my hands over my hair to smooth down the threads that so desperately wanted to be all over the place and exasperated, blew out hot air. I pulled it back into a bun and proceeded to walk out to my room and lotion up.

My eyes zoomed in on a red rose lying on my bed. I stopped in my tracks and called out, "Michael!"

Silence took over the air as I waited on a response. Then I heard him say, "Get dressed. I'm in the living room."

Turning on my heels, I rushed to dress, eager to not only see him, but I felt I could escape into his arms. I needed to cry out on someone's shoulder. Even if we had unresolved issues, I needed someone to hold me and to say it was going to be OK. I didn't have Tionna to call. I didn't want to burden Mama. And my only brother and sister were in D.C. Talk about few options.

I walked into the living room and noticed Michael seated on the far end of my couch. I hadn't seen him awhile. Not since we stood in this very room with Chance right slab in the middle of our confrontation.

"Michael!" I called his name just above a whisper as if I were afraid of him yelling or screaming out of some sort. I sat down on the other end and added, "Thank you for the rose."

"You're welcome. How have you been?" he asked. I looked him over. He was looking quite debonair for early in the morning. He was dressed casually, his hair looked freshly cut, he smelled like desire.

I had hoped I was looking somewhat decent. But all I kept visioning was me looking like a blown-up fat chick that was ready to pop. "I'm been doing . . ." I replied sarcastically. I couldn't say much of anything else as I had been an emotional wreck since the last time I saw him.

He eyed my coffee table and signaled with his body language that he wanted me to look too. "Brought something to you."

I shifted my weight in my seat and saw the piece of paper there. I raised an eyebrow and said, "Oh!" Reaching for it, I flipped it over and casually began to read it.

I suddenly felt the pressure of agony in my throat, as if a small animal was lodged in it, and turned my attention from the piece of paper to him. I looked him over and stared him in his eyes. His almond-colored eyes seemed peaceful, clear, and at ease. I wondered what mine read.

"The kid isn't yours?" I mumbled. "Well, that's good news." I was making a statement, but I was asking him and he knew that.

"It's not news to me; I already knew this information as I have told you for weeks now."

Two months of wondering if Michael was the father of LeAnn's kid were now out the door, but what did that mean for us? It had seemed we were always on an up-and-down roller coaster, and I knew why. Me!

"OK, I'll give you that. That is true. I just didn't know."

"You could have trusted me." He threw up his hands. "Whatever what's done is done. I had no doubts that LeAnn's kid wasn't mine. But now I am faced with another situation."

I set the paper back down on the table and placed my hands in my lap. "Oh? And that is?"

He stood up as my head jerked upward to follow his motions. "I'm not going to say a long speech. It's not needed. Because, to be honest, you have been clear about what you want for months, and I know that it isn't me. You consistently pushed me away for a reason, which I'm not certain of. But I'm tired of the back and forth. I'll be thirty-five soon. I want a woman who will be there for me through thick and thin, and I want to be the best father that I know I can be."

"I'm sure you will be," I added.

"Yeah, that's my point. We have about a month before the baby is here, and I have already put in my request with your doctor for a paternity test."

I yelled, "You did *what?*"

"Brittany, let's not go there. We both know very well that you aren't the most reliable person."

I struggled to stand up. I had to place leverage on a nearby chair, and once I was up, I continued, "Michael, I would never lie to you about this baby."

Michael just stood there and placed his hands in his pockets as if I hadn't just told him I wasn't lying about this baby being his. I didn't like the way he was looking at me. I didn't see the same love he used to have for me there. It was more a look of pity and annoyance.

Oh my God, what have I done? In this very moment, I knew I had taken my antics to the extreme. He was done with me. I could see it in his eyes; he no longer was going to take my bullshit. I had pushed him to his limits.

"Four weeks, Brittany, and we will know," he casually said.

I raised up my right hand as to stop him from talking and stated, "You *are* joking, right? This is payback for my not believing in you. OK, joke over."

"No, Brittany, this isn't a joke. I'm done with your back and forth, done with your allegations, and most of all, Brittany, I'm just done with us. I can't do this anymore. I can't be with someone who consistently pushes me away, doubts my love for her, and not only that, gets involved with someone else."

I raised an eyebrow. "Huh?"

He gave me that *don't play with me* look. "Chance! I heard you talking to yourself in the shower just a minute ago. I know what you meant because I've been there and done that. So I think, what woman gets involved and has sex with another man when she is pregnant by someone else?"

"I . . . I . . ." I stuttered.

"A whore! A conniving, lying whore."

Michael's words were cutting me like a blade. The sharpest blade that man ever created was not piercing through my heart like his words.

He stepped from around the couch and walked toward the front door. My eyes followed him as my mouth was stuck halfway opened. I didn't know what to say. I couldn't say much. He had made his assumptions, and they were straight-on. I couldn't defend my wrongdoing, because it was wrong, and I knew that.

He placed his hands on the doorknob, and then turned to look back at me once more. "Oh, one thing I don't understand."

I stared at him, my eyes full of tears, and I was certain nearly red with embarrassment, fear, and exhaustion, all in one. "What?" I mumbled.

"Your girl Tionna. Yeah, what's interesting about your friend there," he pointed at our college graduation picture, "is that I saw her in the club not even a week ago. Has she called you? You know what? I'm sure she hasn't because she has some agenda going on herself."

"What are you talking about?" I grew weak at the knees from his mysterious comments.

"LeAnn and Tionna. Oh, you didn't know? Maybe you should have paid closer attention to her instead of throwing accusations at me."

"LeAnn and Tionna? I don't get it!"

"They're friends. Something that doesn't make sense."

I grew uneasy from his declaration. No, it didn't make sense. I didn't understand why Tionna would lie about Chance or be caught up with anything LeAnn was trying to do to me.

I felt weak. I reached out to find the arm of my couch to lean on, but missed. I screamed out as I noticed I was plunging to the floor. Michael rushed toward me and caught me midair. I felt the sudden rush of pain in my stomach, then I screamed again.

Michael scooped me up in one swift move and rushed me out the front door. I could only imagine where he was taking me.

LeAnn

I WAS ABOUT bored with the antics. Shit, now was the best time to take that trip to Miami before I was about to pop this baby out. I walked into my closet and looked for the best outfits to wear. The ones I could still fit in.

The buzzing of my phone on vibrate interrupted my quest to attack my closet. I saw her name flash across the screen and said, "Hey, I was just getting ready to call you," I lied.

"So, obviously, Michael knows the kid isn't yours now, right?" Tionna asked.

"Yep. Nothing else to do on this end. I'm going to take that trip I told you about. You wanna come?"

Tionna blew out air in annoyance. "Yeah, I guess so. I'm just about done with this whole thing anyhow. Ready to hit the damn beach myself."

I laughed and said, "I was thinking the same damn thing. Shoot, I got to before this baby comes. Then I know I'll be bored as hell being a mommy and all that extra shit. Anyway, what you got planned for the rest of the day?"

"I don't know, maybe wash a few loads and lounge around the house."

I rolled my eyes. "Don't you be over there acting like a sour puss and shit because you miss your friend. You're the one that wanted to do this damn plan you had me involved in for months now. Get over it. You're starting to bore me."

"Shut up, LeAnn. I am not boring. I should have some male company over here in a bit anyway."

"Who? It better not be my cousin, you ho," I laughed out.

She returned the laugh and said, "No, LeAnn. Damn, I said I'm done with wanting him. I was trying my best to get him back with Brittany. Shit."

"Stop with your lying ass. You was doing that shit so you could finally fuck Michael. You ain't slick, heifer. I know how you operate."

We both laughed when she added, "True. OK, I'm guilty." I heard her pause and say, "Oh, and speaking of the devil, your cousin is here now. I'll call you back later on tonight to discuss the trip to Miami."

"OK, girl, no problem. And tell my cousin Chance I said, 'Hey, now!'" We laughed and hung up the phone. I went back into my closet in search for my Miami gear.

Kyla

THE SUDDEN JERK of my head brought me back to reality. I heard Chris begin to snicker slightly, although the more he tried to cover up the fact he was laughing the louder he got.

"OK, Chris, it isn't that funny."

"I have been watching your head dangle back and forth for ten minutes now. Oh, it was funny."

"How long have we been waiting now?" I asked halfway sleepy and upset that he was still laughing at me.

"Three hours already. I'm hungry." He switched around in his seat and searched underneath it, and then turned to roam his eyes in my backseat.

"What are you looking for?" I asked annoyed at his constant fidgeting.

"Where's the food, Ms. Charlie's Angel. I know you packed something for this high-society stake we are maintaining here. I won't be able to hold on much longer without food."

"Ugh, dang, I don't have anything." I reached into my purse and pulled out a peppermint. "Here you go!"

He raised an eyebrow and said, "Woman, is you serious? You dragged me across town to stake out an apartment to watch whatever is supposed to go down and you didn't pack any food?"

"Like food was the first thing on my mind. Umm . . . no!"

Chris pushed back in his seat and blew out hot air. He was annoyed and upset. Hell, so was I. I was tired of waiting for some action to jump off.

Suddenly, Chris jerked his head up when he saw something interesting. "Look!"

I followed his eyes, and my eyes zoomed in on Krishell walking out of the apartment. She was talking on her cell phone, and it looked as if it was a heated conversation. I wish that I had the talent to read people's lips. Instead, I just read her body movements.

The car was silent. Neither Chris nor I spoke a word as we watched the action that was about to go down. *I needed some answers.* "Why were you two hanging out, Chris?"

I began to think of the obvious now. Why *was* Chris with her? Were they dating? Did he like her?

He turned his body to face me. "I know what you're thinking."

"Do you?" I asked sarcastically.

"No, I wasn't sleeping with her. No, we never kissed. No, I never touched her in a sexual way."

"But you wanted to?"

He grew silent for a couple of minutes before continuing. "Let's call it what it is. You were still with Keith, and you still are, for all I know. So, yeah, I hung out with Krishell, but in spite of that, I never attempted or planned on doing anything with her. But sitting here and saying that, if our routine would have continued like we are now, then I'm sure I would have eventually been interested in her."

"Even after moving here to be with me?" I challenged him.

"Exactly. I moved here to be with you, but for two months now, I've been forced to wait for you to choose between me and someone else. Someone who was . . ." His voice trailed off. He stopped midsentence as if he was hesitating to say the next line.

"What?" I yelled. His attention was derailed back to the apartment. He lifted up his hand and his mouth dropped. It was if he wanted to speak, but the words couldn't escape his mouth.

I turned my head to see what had him shaken. I tilted my head in confusion and squinted my eyes to make sure I was seeing this correctly.

Krishell, Nadine, and there stood Gloria. "What in the world!" I yelled out. I hadn't seen Gloria in weeks. My so-called best friend had totally dropped me. I had no idea why. But seeing her stand next to the mysterious Nadine had me on edge. I was beyond confused.

Nadine placed her hand on Gloria's shoulder as if she was giving her some orders. Gloria nodded her head in a yes-ma'am gesture. I grew annoyed with my confusion and anger. Just as I was reaching for my car door to open it, Chris grabbed my arm.

I jerked my hand toward him and yelled, "Don't!"

"No. You don't want to go over there, Kyla." His eyes showed that he was scared for me. They weren't furious or apologetic for my obvious pain, but it was as if he did not want me to confront this. He then slowly turned his head back toward the group of women . . . and that's when my heart stopped.

My eyes turned red and filled with fury as I saw him step to the women and kiss each of them on their foreheads. I whispered his name as if I had to speak it to believe it. "Keith!"

Michael

I WATCHED BRITTANY wince in pain as they laid her down on the bed and began to hook her up to monitors. One of the lead nurses brought in an ultrasound machine to take a look at the baby. I couldn't lie; I stood there pacing back in forth in the ER room until I was asked to leave so that they could pay closer attention to Brittany without any distractions from me.

They had handed me her belongings. I wanted to reach out to her family, but I didn't feel comfortable in going through her phone. I didn't want to find something I didn't want to see. I went to my phone and texted my brother Omar, my mom, and Ms. Lorraine, asking them to please meet us at Baylor University Hospital.

I knew that I was on edge because of Brittany and my argument only moments before I had to bring her here. I shouldn't have come at her so hard like I did. It's funny how we let our emotions get to us, but to be honest, I wanted to justify my actions.

The thought that she allowed another man inside of her when she was supposedly pregnant with my son sickened me. To be honest, I loved Brittany, but there was no coming back from that. I was done, this was true. But I still had hopes that she was carrying my son. That, I couldn't lie about. I wanted to be a dad.

Half an hour later, the nurse returned. "Her placenta ruptured," she told me. "We will have to keep her here and monitor the baby closely in order for the doctor to decide on what to do next."

I nodded my head that I understood and dropped back down into my seat. They were taking her upstairs. To be honest I was afraid of going up there. What would I say? What do I do? Would she even want me there? I didn't wait to decide on what the answer would be. I went to the gift shop and purchased some flowers, a balloon, and a teddy.

As awkward as it would be, I wanted to bring these things with me to make my entrance into the hospital room easier. I felt the buzz of my cell and read that my brother was here. I blew out hot air in relief and was more comfortable with having another person here with me. I let him know where to meet me.

Once together, he asked how I was holding up.

"You have no idea."

Making my way in to the room I noticed Ms. Lorraine had made it there as well. I walked over to her and kissed her cheek. Afterward, I placed the items I had purchased by the nearby window.

I stuffed my hands in my pocket and nervously looked at Brittany. "How are you feeling?"

She had spoken low and barely made eye contact with me when she said, "Fine! The pain has subsided. I'm good now."

Her voice had trailed off, as if she wanted me to take the hint to leave. I took it and signaled for Omar to meet me outside. "Well, Ms. Lorraine, I'm going to head out." I walked over to her and gave her another kiss on her cheek.

"You're not staying?" she asked confused.

"No, ma'am, I don't want to be here once Chance shows up. Oh, and here are your things, Brittany." I set her phone by the window.

"Chance?" Ms. Lorraine asked, turning from me to Brittany.

I didn't want to answer Ms. Lorraine's question as I proceeded to walk out of the room and quickly jumped into telling Omar what I had learned about Chance and Brittany. "She was with him last night," I declared. I listened to Omar tell me how all women were the same and to move on to the next. I wanted so badly to believe that Omar was wrong, but with Brittany, he was totally right. And moving on was my best bet.

Keith

"LADIES, LOOKING BEAUTIFUL today. Gloria, good to see you're back." I looked over the ladies as I made my way up the stairs and led them back into the apartment.

"So, Gloria is going to meet up with the gentleman S. Frank tonight and R. David tomorrow. We haven't set up the weekend's activities, but I'm on it," Nadine said as we all sat down on the couch. I had nodded at a few other girls who were seated around the house as well.

"Is everything accounted for?" I asked Nadine, referencing the money count.

"Yep, we are set to go. All accounted for," she replied.

"Krishell, you take care of Chris for me?" I asked her.

She shook her head no. "He isn't answering for me now, and tonight was going to be the night I made my move. I'm still on it. It will get done."

"I told you I wanted him out of the picture a long time ago. You're slipping, K. You were one of the best. What happened?"

"I quit the business, that's what happened, Keith. Damn! Don't push me, OK? This is my last favor, and I'm making sure I fulfill it, all right?"

I picked up my cigar Nadine had placed there for me and lit it. Taking three short puffs I nodded my head to her and gestured for her to put a move on it.

"So anyway, I'll see you all next week then," Gloria replied.

I looked toward her and asked, "Are you clean now? I don't want my girls on that shit."

"I'm clean, OK? Don't hound me about it."

I laughed, "You are a fuck up. Even you husband left your trifling ass."

Nadine butted in, "Keith, not now. Gloria, go ahead and leave, and I'll see you tomorrow night for you to cash out."

Gloria grabbed her purse and marched toward the front door and swung it up. Then I heard her scream out, "Oh my God!" as we all rushed to the front door.

The cigar slipped out of my mouth as I said, "Kyla, what are you doing here?"

Krishell plopped down on the couch and casually said, "Well, game over," as she eyed Chris who stood next to Kyla.

I looked around the apartment trying to figure out how to lie my way out of this and said, "I can explain." Kyla threw up her hand and looked from me to Gloria.

"Perhaps my best friend can tell me what the hell is really going on!" Kyla yelled. The room fell silent as all eyes were locked on Gloria.

Gloria

I STEPPED BACK and immediately felt the rush of anxiety. This was not the way for me to finally be free. At this very moment I needed a hit of that good stuff. I needed to drown my sorrows into a pile of that powdery substance. Whatever control it had on me, it did me right. Made me forget about the bad shit I was being forced to do. My whole life was forgotten in those moments. I was free.

I didn't need her looking at me as if she felt sorry for me. "What?" I screamed at her. She jumped at my sudden anger. Who was I kidding? My anger wasn't sudden. It had been here all along.

"Gloria," Kyla called out.

I rolled my eyes and walked away and stood next to Nadine.

Keith chimed in, "Kyla, what are you doing here?" He was torn between embarrassment and anger I could tell. I knew his tone when he wasn't pleased. I knew it all too well.

Kyla walked through the door with Chris, who was looking around the room. "It's a whorehouse!" He wasn't asking. He was proclaiming. Krishell jumped up from her seat when he said that. Her reaction was shocking to me. Nadine and I frowned at her.

"Calm down, Krishell," Nadine ordered nonchalantly.

"Chris, how did you even know to come here?" Krishell asked. I was curious too. Ironically, I would have thought Kyla's eyes would have been glued to Keith. After all, he was the one she was with, well, until recently, I guess. No matter what I would do to Keith and for him, I was never his chosen one. However, her eyes were stuck on me; her eyes were sad. She was sad. I grew confused.

"What are you staring at, Ky?" My Spanish tongue was strong and slurred. You could barely tell exactly what I was saying.

"What happened to you? What the hell did they do to you?"

I could tell Kyla wanted to walk over to me. She seemed to want to console me, and that made me even more confused. Why did she care?

"Don't act like you care about me," I screamed back.

"We've been following you for a while . . . well, she has," Chris said to Krishell about Kyla. "And today of all days we find all the pieces to this hidden puzzle in one place. What I don't understand is why, who, when, where, and what the fuck," Chris added.

"Lower your tone in this house," Keith demanded. Chris made a step toward him in a gesture to fight, but Kyla held up her hand to stop him in midstride.

"Explain. Someone say something," Kyla screamed.

Chris interjected and added, "For one, Keith and Gloria were sleeping together, that I knew but didn't know how to tell you."

Kyla's head jerked from Chris to me to Keith.

"You did *what?*" Kyla's eyes were burning into Keith's flesh. He grew uncomfortable and tried to explain himself in so many words. Kyla added, "You two were together?"

Nadine cut in, "Baby girl, calm down. I am his wife; this thing here is simply one of his toys, as were you." I winced at her referencing me as a toy.

"What the hell?" Chris added.

Frustrated, Kyla ran her fingers through her hair and shook her head as if she was attempting to shake a bug away. "You're married and were sleeping with my best friend?"

My heart fluttered when I heard Kyla call me her best friend. "You took advantage of Gloria? You were lying to me? You said you wanted us to be together." Nadine's weight shifted from one leg to the other as her attention was now set on Keith.

Nadine turned back to Kyla and spoke for Keith. "You were just his toy, baby girl," she smirked.

Krishell threw up her hands and screamed, "Enough!" He eyes zoomed in on Chris and if I was correct, I could tell that Krishell was feeling Chris in more ways than she was supposed to. "Chris, Kyla, this is the deal. Keith employed us. I used to be one of his girls. I no longer am, but from time to time I may do a job for them. Chris was a job, to deflect his attention from you to me so that Keith could have you."

Chris and Kyla stood there stunned, and as they took in more of Krishell's declaration, I saw the hurt in Kyla's eyes. And my confusion was now boiling over. I interjected, "Why do you seem so hurt, Kyla? You didn't care about me; you just wanted me gone."

"Who told you that?" Kyla asked.

My eyes darted toward Nadine, who then laughed and said, "Gloria, you will believe *anything.*" Her laughter continued, and with each chuckle, I felt my heart break, my spirit broken, and I was beyond the point of returning to normal. *My life, my marriage, my job, my friendships, and my body have been taken by this woman and Keith.*

I ran into the kitchen and pulled out Keith's gun that he kept in the top drawer for protection. "I'm going to kill you!" I screamed out. I didn't hear the screams and commotions around me as I pointed the gun toward my main target. Nadine. Then I pulled the trigger. I felt a rush of release escape my body.

Brittany

MAMA STOMPED INTO my hospital room and plopped down on the chair. She turned up the volume and focused her attention on the TV. She hadn't said much of anything since Michael left, telling her the obvious, that I was with Chance.

I was embarrassed and hurt at the same time. I didn't know what to say so I didn't say anything. "Mama?" I called out.

"Shut up, Brittany, you are interrupting my show." I sighed deeply and turned my attention toward the window where I focused in on the bear and balloon Michael had purchased. The regret I was beginning to have was wearing thin on me. I quickly wiped away the tear that found itself onto my cheek.

"No need for tears now. You got what you wanted. A good man gone," Mama yelled out. Her voice held no sympathy.

"Mama, I don't need the extra," I whined.

"No, what you need is an ass whopping. Shit. Dumb-ass little girl playing games with a grown man. I swear I don't know where I went wrong with you," Mama continued.

I didn't reply. I was hoping she had the answer about why I was this way. No friends, no man, no nothing. A measly career because I didn't know what I wanted to do with my life . . . and now this. I succeeded at becoming a single mother.

"Did you call Kyla?" I asked.

"Yep, she didn't answer. I don't blame her. This mess you got yourself into. But I'm sure once she gets my message she and your brother Sean will be on their way. Look, I'm upset with you but don't stress over what I'm saying. Just me venting and wishing I could physically beat your behind for pushing that boy away." Mama rose up from her seat and headed toward the door. "I'm going to go get you some food from the cafeteria. Rest up."

I nodded my head OK and closed my eyes as she walked out.

"Brit Brat," I heard the voice of Mr. Familiar. I opened my eyes and smiled.

I then returned his gesture and said, "Chance, you can't be here." I glanced over his shoulder to see Michael standing there.

"Just the two people I wanted to talk to." This was the opposite of rest as I prepared myself for whatever Michael had to say.

Kyla

GROANING, I TURNED on my right side and squeezed my eyes real tight. I heard the sudden clash and jumped up from where I was lying. Screaming out, I heard footsteps run up to me. "Sorry, babe, I dropped one of those coffee cups."

My head was ringing. I barely opened my eyes to focus in on Chris because the light that was on was piercing my pupils. I heard a door open, and then a familiar voice.

"Baby girl, are you awake now?" The sound of Sean's voice, my big brother. I smiled slightly and nodded my head like I as a school-age girl.

My mouth was dry as I managed to speak. "Why am I sleeping on a chair in your detective's office?" My brother, being a cop and ex-military, currently had a detective position at a precinct in D.C. He was one of the reasons why I came out here to go to

Howard once I graduated high school. He was my only other family here.

Chris and Sean fell quiet until Chris said, "Just about twelve hours ago we ran into Gloria, remember?"

I looked at him questioningly. Then the mention of Gloria's name reminded me of the events only hours ago. "She's dead," I whispered. Chris sat down next to me and began to massage my shoulder.

"We've gotten the statements from everyone at the house. An arrest has been made, sis. The only thing for you to do is go home now. I'm going to come over later. The wife, the kids, and I will spend the night."

I jerked at the flashing image of Gloria placing that shiny silver in her mouth and pulling the trigger. "Arrest?" I mumbled and looked up toward Sean who was standing over me.

Chris interjected, "Keith and Nadine. They ran a whorehouse, Kyla." I dropped my head and swallowed hard. I squeezed my eyes really tight, and then peeked out of my left one. No, I was still there. It wasn't a dream.

I asked Sean, "Did you find her husband Victor?"

He nodded yes. "But he isn't coming in town till this weekend. He moved to Chicago three months ago."

I dropped my head and covered my face with my hands. Victor had been gone for months. I cried at the idea of what my friend was going through, and I didn't even know it.

Chris embraced me and said, "Babe, when you were asleep, Sean got a text from Mama Lorraine." I looked up at him as he continued. I was hoping it wasn't more bad news. "Brit is in the hospital. She may deliver any day now."

Sean added, "Do you want to go there? Do you want to go back to Fort Worth and take some time off?"

I nodded my head yes again. Brittany was heavy on my mind now. The thought of my nephew coming into this world without my being there now had me paining in my chest. "Book my flight. I don't need to take anything but my purse and the clothes on my back."

Chris got up as quickly as he could and marched over to a computer nearby. Sean looked at me and said, "I'm coming with you, sis. It's going to be OK." He kissed my cheek and walked over to his desk and picked up the phone. "Hey, Mama, yes, it's me. I'm coming home. All of us. Yes, some time tomorrow. OK, yes. Love you too."

I lay my head back down and begged for some more headache medicine to help knock me out. I really didn't want to go to sleep until the pill had taken control of my body, mind, and spirit.

Michael

SOMETHING WASN'T RIGHT about Chance. I just didn't know what, but I didn't have time to worry about that. Today was the day. The baby was in distress, and they eventually broke Brittany's water to initiate her labor. Brittany was having the baby tonight. It was less than 48 hours ago when we stood in her living room having the mother of all fights, and now it was time for the baby to be born. I so badly wanted to say my son, but even after talking to Chance, I wasn't sure.

"Just leave," Brittany moaned out in between her labor pains. She was directing her aggression toward Chance who was begging to stay to support her. I wanted to punch the shit out of him. It wasn't helping either that Omar was egging me on to do just that.

With my own mother and Mama Lorraine at Brittany's bedside giving her ice chips and placing cold towels on her head, there wasn't much for me to do.

Mama Lorraine's eyes darted toward Chance. "She doesn't want you here now, so you can return after the baby is born."

I so badly wanted Chance to say something back to Mama Lorrain. Something disrespectful so I could punch the shit out of him. But he nodded, bowed his head, and waltzed his ass out.

The veins in my forehead were creating a scene. Everyone within five feet of me knew I was beyond upset. Hell, I was embarrassed; Brittany was making a fool of me.

Mama Lorraine looked at me and said, "I'm sorry, son."

I dryly replied, "Mama, you didn't do anything, I mean, we are in a sticky situation. I'm here just for support and the test."

I heard Brittany suck her teeth and groan. "What the hell are you smoking? This kid is yours."

I didn't bother to reply. My mama looked at me and said, "Son, it's going to be a long night. You and Omar go for a walk."

I got up and followed her orders as Omar placed a hand on my shoulder and leaned to my ear and whispered, "We still got time to follow Chance and beat that ass."

I replied, "I ain't got to fight over no female, man, and I ain't going to start today."

Kyla

I FOLLOWED THE pattern on the white floor on the labor and delivery ward. I was gripping the purse strap on my shoulder as my current source of relief. "This way," Chris led.

I read the numbers on the hospital walls: 7, 9, 11, and 13. I walked through the door and saw Mama rubbing Brittany's temple. "Brit Brat!"

Brittany looked toward me and stretched out her hands. Mama's eyes watered up as the beginning of her tears began to flow. Sean, his wife, and kids all followed in, first going to Mama and surrounding her with hugs and kisses. The scene was beautiful, just like I had imagined it would be. I squeezed and kissed on Mama and Brittany so much that I forgot Brittany was in labor for that split second.

"Well, how dilated are ya, heifer?" I screamed out in excited.

Brittany tilted her head and looked at me with so much concern that I began to frown and asked, "What's wrong, baby girl?"

"Your eyes. They look so sad. What's wrong, what happened?" Brittany asked.

I waved her off and smiled through my tears. "I'm just so happy to see you, Brit, and for baby Michael to be here." I rubbed her belly. Then I turned and introduced myself to a woman I came to know as Michael's mom. Then I asked, "Where's Michael?" The room fell silent. I eyed Brittany and added, "So that's the word I've been missing."

Mama added, "You missed a lot, Kyla." She turned to everyone and shooed them out of the room. I took my attention back to Brittany, whom I could tell was beginning to feel the drugs take effect as she began to doze off.

"Just go on to sleep, sis. We don't have to worry about talking about Michael or anything else. Just you get ready to bring my nephew on home." I took a towel and began to wipe her brow and sing to her. I don't know what song I was singing, I just let the words flow.

When I heard a slight knock on the door I turned and saw Michael walking through and smiled curiously. "Well, you're the mystery man of the hour." I got up, walked over to him, and whispered some quick words. We gave each other an embrace.

"I'm sure you are out of the loop, but I'm here to support your sis. I'm a man of my word," he whispered back.

His tone gave me the hint that something was done to him and not the other way around. I didn't ask any questions. I just nodded my head OK. "Do you want to sit next to her?" He nodded his head yes and took a seat next to me. In return, he began to tell me why Brittany and he were at odds, and I began to explain how I was here only hours after witnessing my best friend commit suicide.

He paused, looked at me, and then back to Brittany, and said, "Damn, forget my mess. Let me allow you to vent." And even though I didn't know Michael, I used him as my temporary shoulder to lean on and told him my story.

Krishell

I TURNED AND looked at my apartment one last time as one of the movers walked by me and asked me if there was anything else I needed. I assured him I was OK as I gave them more instructions on relocating my things to my next destination. I had my move day planned out ever since Nadine asked me to woo Chris. I had planned on moving far away from her and Keith's grip long ago.

With them both currently sitting in jail awaiting arraignment on their sex charges I put my escape plans in action.

I had only wished I had time to say good-bye to Chris so I wrote him a letter instead and bid him farewell. Glad that my plan with him didn't go that far, I was happy too for him and Kyla and whatever they had planned on doing together. The heck if I knew or cared.

I walked outside and handed my personal bags to the cabdriver and took one more look around me. I had always wanted to move out west. L.A. was calling my name.

I turned on my heels and marched toward the cab and got in. I was ready to start something new. To finally fall in love and to finally move on. The past was just that—the past. As far as I cared, it never existed.

Chance

I PULLED UP in front of LeAnn's house to catch her before she left. I knocked on her door, and she swung it open. "Fool, what the hell? Why are you banging on my door as if you are the police?"

I marched in and said, "Trying to catch Tionna and you before y'all left for Miami."

Tionna walked in from the back of LeAnn's house and asked, "Here, what's up? Do not be longwinded. We're about to head to the airport."

I was marching back and forth, nervous and anxious at the same time. "Brittany is about to give birth."

LeAnn laughed and walked past me, pushing me on my shoulder jokingly. "Boy, I thought something *serious* was going on. Of course she's giving birth; she's pregnant. Duh!"

"No, she is in labor now, at this very moment."

Tionna paused from looking in the mirror to put on her lipstick and said, "Oh, well, that's good for her." I could hear the regret in her voice when she spoke.

"T, you want me to take you up there?"

She swung around angrily and yelled, "Now why would I do that when she knows I lied on you and broke y'all up? Fool, please go away with this mess. I'm good. I'm headed to Miami."

"I figured we could try to fix y'all or something. Explain it and show that I forgive you. Then I know Brittany and I will be together."

The girls rolled their eyes and laughed. LeAnn added, "Cousin, sorry to tell you, but I don't know about that. What will you do? Hide me forever? When she finds out about me, she's going to cut your dick off."

"She ain't ever going to see your trifling ass, LeAnn," I barked back.

The girls laughed in unison and began to pick up their bags and walk toward me, "Look, Cousin, we got a plane to catch. Good luck though. No, really wishing you the best." She blew me an arrogant kiss into the wind and walked past me.

Tionna walked by me still in laughter. I heard LeAnn call out, "Fool, bring your ass on so I can lock my door."

I walked out of her house and stormed angrily to my car. I was still where I was in the beginning: stuck on how to get Brittany back.

Brittany

I GRUNTED TO clear my throat. "Nurse, give me some water," I whined. She happily obliged my request and handed me some of the best ice-cold water a girl could ever ask for. I took a swig and exhaled. Immediately, I winced as I felt pain in my bosom.

"Still feeling those contractions, huh?" the nurse asked.

"I thought that mess was over after the baby was born."

"No, ma'am, you may feel this for a couple more days here and there as your cervix goes back to its original size. But I will order up some more pain meds for you."

I nodded my head and looked toward the bassinet. "Where is MJ?" I searched the room and noticed Michael sound asleep and smiled when I saw baby MJ sleeping on his chest.

"I'll go get the baby and put him back in his bed," the nurse said.

I suddenly started to hear the melody of Tony! Toni! Toné!

Just give me all your lovin', girl, after all the rubbin'

That's all I ask of you

I'll kiss you anywhere, yes, love, even there

That's all I ask of you

Kissin' you is not enough for me

You know I'm a big boy and big boys have desires

Makin' love is what I wanna do

But I need a true friend to make it come together

Just give me all your lovin', girl, after all the rubbin'

That's all I ask of you

I'll kiss you anywhere, yes, love, even there

That's all I ask of you

Laughing I attempted to sit up as I saw Michael shuffle around in his seat. Suddenly his eyes popped open, and he went in search of the baby when he noticed he was no longer on his chest.

I heard Kyla's laughter as the music lowered. I whispered, "Are you the DJ now?"

"Just trying to get the loving back in this room flowing. I'm going to take my nephew over here and leave you two alone." She set the iPod down on the table beside me and pushed the bassinet out of the room with MJ in tow.

Michael chuckled as he began to wipe the sleep out of his eyes. "So, you're going to name him MJ?" he asked after stretching as he made his way over to my bed.

"Might as well. I mean, you are his daddy." I looked away and focused my attention off of Michael and added, "Did you test him?"

There was a short pause, and then he replied, "Yes, Brittany, I did."

I fought the tears that were fighting their way to the surface as I whispered, "I'm sorry."

Placing his hand on my shoulder, he gave it a tight squeeze but didn't say a word. I didn't understand Michael sometimes. Even now he was warm and caring. Shoot, I don't blame him for testing MJ. That I would give him and not argue with him about.

"It's all going to work out," Michael added. I placed my hand on top of his and nodded my head OK.

Kyla

I WAS STRETCHED across Brittany's full-size bed in her old room at Mama Lorraine's house finally trying to get some shut-eye. My brain was still in overdrive as I got random voice mails from coworkers trying to be nosey and give condolences at the same time. I shut my phone off just as Chris walked back in to ask if I was all right.

I hadn't slept in a day. Brittany and MJ were resting, and Michael was at her side, which I appreciated. Mama was downstairs, more likely cooking up a huge breakfast. "I'm fine," I mumbled and rolled over. He placed a kiss on my forehead.

"I went to go see my daughter, and then to my mom's house. She told Dean that we were here."

I rolled my eyes at the mention of Dean, my ex and Chris's brother's name. "Oh, did she?"

"Yeah, so I am over here hiding from what I know is going to be an interrogation from my brother," Chris said, plopping down on the bed beside me. I heard Sean call out from downstairs that the food was ready.

"OK," I yelled.

"I miss this," I laughed.

"What?"

"Waiting in my room for Mama to call me down to come eat. Shoot, the way I'm feeling, I'm thinking of just staying up here in Brittany's old room forever."

"That's hiding, babe."

"I know." I shrugged. "I just want to hide right now. Then I won't have to think about Glo . . ." My words trailed off. "Nothing. Let's just go eat."

Chris grabbed my wrist and said, "D.C. Do you want to return there?"

I paused and sighed, "Nothing is there anymore. I shouldn't go back."

"Do you want to?" he asked again. I allowed the question to dance around in my head. For over a decade I had focused on school, then my career, forgetting about home, family, and the possibility of love. The first man I seriously dated in D.C. ends up being the man who tricked out my best friend and turned her into a ho. I lost her because of him, and now the walls of my office will remind me every day of that.

I fell back into Chris's arms and stretched my legs across the bed. "Nope, I do not want to go back," I announced.

"Then we won't go back. I'll fly back, pack up all your things, and have them shipped to Texas. You just worry about being happy and being my lady."

I laughed and couldn't help but smile. "Your lady? OK, I like that idea."

Epilogue

Tionna

I WALTZED BACK into my apartment after a weeklong vacation to Miami, and lo and behold, Chance is sitting on my front step. I wasn't in the mood for one of his begging spells of "help me get Brittany back." I was over it. I had to be, and there was no going back. Nothing I could do now anyway. I had betrayed her, and she knew that.

"Negro, go home," I said dropping my bags by my feet to open my front door.

Chance followed me inside of my house pretending to help me as he placed my bags on my living-room floor. "Did you enjoy Miami?"

"Yep, now what's up?"

He chuckled and said, "Straight to the point, huh?"

I rolled my eyes and replied yes as I sorted through my mail. "Come on, Chance, what do you want?"

"Brittany won't take my calls. I need you to call her for me."

I dropped the mail on the table, "Look, it's over. Brittany and Michael have a baby now. It's his kid, OK? Get over it. I'm done fucking with her. Ain't no good going to come from that."

"You're the reason why I'm not with her anyway," Chance shot back. I gave him the Idon'tgiveafuck look.

"If I walk away I gave up," Chance cried out.

I rolled my eyes and said, "Plan didn't work. I didn't get an opportunity to even seduce Michael like I wanted to. The kid is his, the plan with LeAnn died quickly, the shit is over. Move on."

Chance hopped up from where he was seated and cried out, "I see where you're at. Always so damn selfish."

"Duh, this is *me*. Ms. Selfish. Now bye."

Chance turned around to walk out but stopped in his tracks. I switched my hips from one leg to the other and folded my arms across my chest to show attitude and barked, "What?"

He turned around, smiled, then licked his lips and asked, "Since what's done is done, why don't you get what you been waiting for all these years anyway?"

I raised an eyebrow and looked him over. Was he for real? This fool was throwing his dick at me like it was a wand.

"Are you serious?"

He slowly walked over to me as I stayed planted in my spot and trailed his finger from my waistline to the bare skin of my breast that was peeking through the buttons of my blouse.

"Dead serious! Now strip."

A seductive smirk spread thin across my face as I allowed him to unbutton my blouse one button at a time. A perfect ending to this story, huh? Well, at least for me. I actually got some dick out of this.

Cookie Too: Lyric's Song

Coming Spring 2013

Prologue

I CURSED UNDER my breath as I made my way across the *7 Eleven* parking lot. One thing for sure I was glad it wasn't as cold as it was yesterday and the winter air was actually cool. I was in an ok mood anyhow since I had just had sex with Donnell. That's what I was doing before I was succumbed to go to work to make 500 buttered biscuits. I didn't get paid enough for this annoying shit. This was my day off. ++

I inhaled deep to try to tackle my aggravation and make my way across the parking lot. It was the weekend and it looked like everyone had somewhere to go. I for one had to go into Beefy Burger to work. I sighed jumping at the sight of a roach as big as my finger crawl across my path. I dodge it and cringe.

"Hey!" I yelled out tapping the side of a car. Now *I know he see me standing here.* I took my attention away from that nasty ass bug and back to what was current at hand. Some idiot in his car had done cut me off. Stuck between a rusty car and a parked car I tried to manure out of the way so that he could drive by and I could continue my walk to the bus stop.

His dumb ass finally decided to drive off after he couldn't find whatever he was looking for in his car. Then I felt a tug on my leg. *What the…*

Looking down I tried to find what had a hook on my pants when the tugging increased. *Oh shit my leg is stuck.* Realizing that the rusty car had a metal stick coming out that caught hold of my pants I slam my hands on the side door of his car to alert him to stop.

Pressing my weight on the car I hurriedly tried to pull my leg when the driver started to speed off. Falling down onto my back I yelled out, "Hold up!"

I try to sit up in the same motion you would act out if you were doing stomach crunches and tried to reach for my pants but glancing to my left I see his back tire. My legs completely under his car now, I see the tires motion closing in toward me. I fall back to try to slide from underneath only to feel the massive weight of the car drive over my stomach.

I scream out in agony as I clinched my abdomen so tight I forgot to breathe out. The car completely stopped as I tried to yell over his engine. My leg was finally free, but I felt that my insides were slowly dissolving into puddy as I tried to lean over to lessen the pain.

I see a bright red light to my right, *are they about to back up?* The car's reverse lights beamed into my eye sight when I saw it motioning backwards I hysterically rolled over hoping to get away but when I felt a piercing shot go through my back I knew I didn't move fast enough.

Suddenly my head was slammed down on the ground, my body tossing to its left side as I could hear a blast inside of my head. I squeezed my eyes closed tight and balled up my fist to take the pain, when I realized his back tire began to run directly over my head. I screamed out stop. My voice was groggy and hoarse as I felt a rush of salty liquid form around my mouth. *Blood.*

I felt my back sink in as another tire attacked it and felt my bones crack. The sound of my bone breaking caused me to shiver in fear and use all of my strength to bring the only power I possessed into my voice. I heard people screaming around me, "Hey stop that car!"

As if I peed on myself a gush of warmth passed down my leg as I felt my right leg break slicing my skin in half as the bone made its way into the surface. I felt the car drive forward again connecting its tires with my side causing my entire body to roll over on my back.

I gave up. I could no longer fight the urge to squeeze tight so that the pain wouldn't hurt. I allowed the tightness in my neck to subside, my hands to let loose, and body to lay limp. I had given in; I no longer could get myself free.

I felt someone grab my hands pulling me from underneath the heavy metal asking if I could hear them. I could but I chose not to talk. It hurt too much to even think. I had given in. Maybe after all the shit I've done in my life this was it. Payback for doing wrong. My time had finally come and God was done giving me chances. Shit who could blame him, I ain't did too much of anything good in my life. And now here I lay only a matter of blocks away from where I grew up, laying in my own blood. Dying.

I always imagined that when it was my time, that I would remember everything thing I learned about in *Higher Touch*, that the shouting, praying, and crying would help me get to heaven. Would that work right now? Would God say Lyric James, bring yourself here child. It's time for you to come home. I doubted it; I just knew God was going to turn me away.

Why wouldn't he? If Mama was here she would say, "Lyric gets your life together. No weapon formed against you shall prosper. You hear me?" But she wasn't here saying that. Instead I was dying in my own blood on this cold cement.

If I would have had it my way, I would have said that I went to college, got married, had kids, and was a church going woman who did no wrong. Instead I lived the life of a hustler, chasing fast money, sex, drugs, and alienating everyone around me who ever loved me. Shit I even did some time in prison. But maybe God will overlook all that and let me into heaven. But as I lay here now hearing my own heart beat slow down all I can think of is, was it too late to repent? Could I hurry up and say God forgive me and then suddenly see an Angel reaching out for me. Maybe I should try it really quick.

Wait, maybe, just maybe I'll make it.

CPSIA information can be obtained at www.ICGtesting.com
Printed in the USA
BVOW02s2146210115

384421BV00001B/32/P